If you enjoyed the way Conlan Fox was conquered by love in *Moon of the Raven*, you'll delight in watching the mighty Steven Armstrong fall. Don't miss *Gypsy Moon*, coming in October, where another Armstrong man will meet his match.

## "Forget It, Lady. You're Not Touching My Poor Posterior Ever Again."

With a provocative gleam in her eyes, Samantha teased, "Not ever?"

Steven was about to retract his hasty words, but as soon as the kids saw Samantha open the picnic basket they came out of the bushes at a dead run. "Maybe sometime," he conceded. With a sigh of frustration he added, "But unfortunately, not now."

"Looks like they've worked up quite an appetite," Samantha said as sandwich wrappers went flying.

Steven's dark eyes sparkled with promise as he gazed down at her smiling face. "Not as big as mine."

Samantha's face went hot as she reached to offer him a sandwich and his eyes feasted on the curve of her breast. "Maybe this will tide you over."

Steven took a huge bite, swallowed, then shook his head. "Not for long, Samantha. I'm a very hungry man."

Dear Reader:

Welcome! You hold in your hand a Silhouette Desire—your ticket to a whole new world of reading pleasure.

A Silhouette Desire is a sensuous, contemporary romance about passions, problems and the ultimate power of love. It is about today's woman—intelligent, successful, giving—but it is also the story of a romance between two people who are strong enough to follow their own individual paths, yet strong enough to compromise, as well.

These books are written by, for and about every woman that you are—wife, mother, sister, lover, daughter, career woman. A Silhouette Desire heroine must face the same challenges, achieve the same successes, in her story as you do in your own life.

The Silhouette reader is not afraid to enjoy herself. She knows when to take things seriously and when to indulge in a fantasy world. With six books a month, Silhouette Desire strives to meet her many moods, but each book is always a compelling love story.

Make a commitment to romance—go wild with Silhouette Desire!

Best,

Isabel Swift
Senior Editor & Editorial Coordinator

# JOYCE THIES
# Reach for the Moon

Silhouette Desire

Published by Silhouette Books New York

**America's Publisher of Contemporary Romance**

SILHOUETTE BOOKS
300 East 42nd St., New York, N.Y. 10017

ISBN: 0-373-05444-0

First Silhouette Books printing August 1988

Printed in the U.S.A.

**Books by Joyce Thies**

Silhouette Desire

* *Territorial Rights* #147
*Spellbound* #348
*False Pretenses* #359
*The Primrose Path* #378
†*Moon of the Raven* #432
†*Reach for the Moon* #444

*written as Melissa Scott
†Rising Moon Series

---

## JOYCE THIES

has authored or co-authored over twenty contemporary and historical novels. Readers might recognize her as the Joyce half of Janet Joyce. She wrote her first Silhouette Desire, *Territorial Rights*, as Melissa Scott, but is now writing under her own name.

While researching a historical about early Montana, Joyce fell in love with the beautiful philosophies held by the Absaroka Indian tribe and wanted to share them with her contemporary readers. While studying the memoirs of Plenty Coups, the last legitimate chieftain of the Absaroka, she was inspired to begin the "Rising Moon" series.

To his biographer, Plenty Coups said, "All my life I have tried to learn as the chickadee learns, by listening, so that I might help my people. We love our country because it is beautiful and because we were born here. Remember this, Sign Talker, you have felt my heart and I have felt yours. I want to learn all I can from the white man, for riding with the whirlwind instead of opposing it, we shall save the heartland of our country."

When she read this, Joyce felt the pride and dignity of the Absaroka heart and wished to do as Plenty Coups asked Sign Talker, "To write with a straight tongue so your people shall come to know mine."

# TALES OF THE RISING MOON—BOOK II

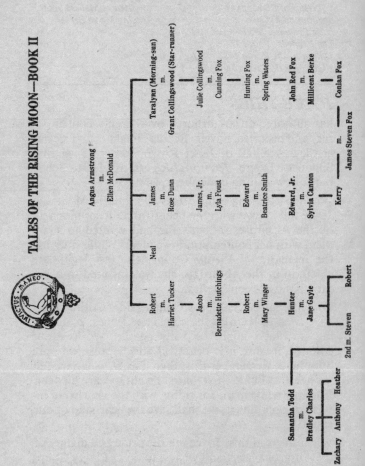

# Prologue

---

**W**ithout warning, a dark rack of clouds rose up on the horizon. Having lived in the shadow of the Rockies all of his life, Steven Armstrong knew what was coming and cursed himself for being caught unawares. Even though spring had arrived early this year, he knew better than to ride out this far on the open range without carrying the proper gear, and he was about to pay for his foolhardy blunder. The marauding pack of wolves he was tracking would find refuge long before he escaped the violent bluster from the oncoming howler.

"Which goes to show that they're one hell of a lot smarter than you," Steven muttered, thoroughly frustrated by the number of times he and the wolves had crossed paths today without his being able to get off a single decent shot. Now, because of his own stupidity, he had much more to worry about than a few slain cattle. Now, his own neck was at stake.

Bracing himself for the first blast of snow, Steven guided his horse toward the timberline. If he kept close to the trees, he might make it to shelter before he lost all sense of direction. The stallion under him covered the distance in less than a minute, as if his instinct for self-preservation was just as strong as his rider's.

Reining in beneath the tall branches of jack pine, Steven untied his neckerchief and used it to secure his hat on his head. After knotting the ends under his chin, he pulled the brim of his Stetson down low over the sides of his face and the back of his neck. His sheepskin-lined jacket would protect his upper body from the cold for a while. Not so the well-worn denim that covered his legs, nor the rawhide gloves that would stiffen up as quickly as the temperature was dropping.

With chilling certainty Steven knew that he had only limited time before he and his horse would be lost in the swirling fury of an invisible cyclone. Once more he urged the stallion into a gallop, but the clouds swiftly outdistanced them, unleashing blinding bursts of snow that came at them from every direction. In a matter of seconds, Steven was hard put to see more than a foot in front of his face.

As his hands and legs lost feeling, Steven lost track of time. Head down, nostrils flaring, the stallion forged ahead, needing no instructions from his rider to tell him that stopping would mean a swift burial for them both. With Steven slung low over his neck, the valiant animal pressed on through the mounting drifts of snow that seemed to build out of nothing into heights of half a man.

Completely disoriented, Steven couldn't tell if he'd gone blind from the repeated onslaught of wind-driven snow upon his face, or if there really was nothing in sight but an unending curtain of white. He tried to find some fixed point to guide him, but his lashes kept freezing over his tearing eyes. Ice-driven whips lashed his body, and his legs were already numb from the continuous beating. He'd hoped to gain some protection by staying close to the trees, but they'd disappeared along with everything else.

For the first time since the freakish storm had begun, he felt real fear and sensed it in his floundering animal, but the emotion was barely compelling enough to override another longing. He desired nothing more than to give in to the lethargy closing in on him. It would be so easy. All he had to do was close his eyes and keep them closed.

Nature was graciously offering him the perfect means to escape the cold and his fear, but something deep inside him refused the offer. Like all the Armstrongs before him, he wasn't the kind to give up without a fight, even when he was up against seemingly impossible odds. "C'mon, boy," he urged through frozen lips, knowing his life depended on the rapidly waning strength of his mount. "We can do it."

Dredging up the stubborn will that was the hallmark of his family, he patted the stallion's neck and tightened his stiff fingers on the ice-coated reins. "We're in this fight together, and we're going to win it or die trying."

# One

The thin walls of the small house shook from the force of the wind, and the single-paned windows rattled. Using her thumbnail, Samantha Charles scraped away several layers of frost from the glass and peered out into the darkness. Since the moon was obscured by heavy clouds, the only illumination was provided by the large beacon mounted on the barn roof, and even that high-powered light was dimmed by the thick boreal veil of wind-whipped flakes.

The early shoots of spring grass coming up in the yard were already buried under a foot of snow, with more falling all the time. She couldn't stay inside much longer. Getting from the house to the barn was going to be difficult; however, Samantha had no choice but to go. Her best cow was in labor, and she couldn't afford to wait until tomorrow to see if the calf survived.

She and the children were dependent on the continued good health of their stock, and with two other heifers down with some unknown ailment, their livelihood was in jeopardy.

As she'd been doing more and more lately, Samantha wondered if her decision to quit her dead-end job at the bank and put all her efforts and savings into making this section of prime Montana grazing land a small, self-sustaining ranch had been a good one. As the daughter of a small-time rancher, she'd known how much work was involved in owning one, but the dividends had seemed well worth it. Instead of working for someone else, she would be working for herself, and she knew there was no better place than a ranch to raise strong, happy, self-reliant children. However, after nine long months, she was no longer so certain that would be the case.

Her enthusiasm was definitely beginning to wane, and the benefits she'd wished for her children were negligible at best. Self-reliance wouldn't fill empty stomachs, and happiness didn't automatically follow landownership. Unfortunately the work involved in running a ranch was harder than she'd remembered and the payoffs less. She'd known that she wouldn't see any profits from her efforts the first year, but she hadn't planned on so many setbacks, either. She'd already used up all the money she'd garnered from the sale of her house in Butte, but the roof was still leaking, her late-summer vegetable garden had failed to produce enough food to carry them through the winter, and the ancient, oil-burning furnace was falling down on the job.

This blizzard seemed the final straw in a series of events that were making her life that much more difficult. She didn't know what she was going to do if the furnace decided to give up the ghost altogether. She couldn't afford to buy a new one, yet neither could she let her children freeze.

This morning she'd given thanks for the prematurely warm weather that allowed her to postpone making such a large purchase for several more months, but just a few hours later, she was again staring that daunting prospect in the face. The only way she could afford such an expenditure was to sell off some stock, and with three of her ten animals already at risk, she might not have that much left to sell.

"So stop dragging your feet and get out to the barn. You need both the mother and her new calf," Samantha reminded herself, turning away from the window and walking toward the curtain that separated the living area and kitchen from the sleeping section of the small house.

Pushing the curtain aside, she saw three pairs of closed eyes and three small, towheaded bodies cuddled close together in the double bed. They were all snoring. "I'm so lucky to have such good children," she murmured, smiling down on their sweet, all-innocence faces. "I tell them it's bedtime, and my little angels go right to sleep."

The snores doubled in volume.

Samantha leaned over the lumpy mattress and slipped her hand under the covers, ignoring the giggles she heard as she extracted a small bag of penny candy, a partially eaten cookie and a bulky toy truck

filled with soda crackers. Further investigation produced a flashlight, several slices of bread, a jar of
peanut butter and a spilled can of grape juice. If not
for the growing wet spot in the center of the mattress,
she might have gathered up all the contraband without comment, but with so little heat in the house, the
sheets would have to be changed.

Someone deserved a good scolding, but Samantha
didn't have the heart to deliver one. As far as she was
concerned, taking away the covers that warmed the
guilty party was punishment enough for both him and
his fellow cohorts in crime. Zack, the eldest of her six-
year-old twins, obviously thought so, too, for as
expected, he was the first to protest.

"Mo...om!" he squealed in indignation, scram-
bling up on his flannel-covered knees. "You're freezing us."

"I'd be happy to warm all your bottoms for you if
that would help," Samantha threatened without much
heat as she quickly stripped away the wet bedding and
tossed it into the large laundry basket placed on the
floor next to the dresser. Next, she pulled open the top
drawer and lifted out a clean sheet. "You know the
rules about eating in bed."

"Nuhuh," four-year-old Heather denied, then
quickly thrust a pudgy thumb back into her mouth as
her mother sent her a stern glance.

The most obedient of the shivering threesome
hopped off the bed to help as Samantha unfolded the
new sheet and shook it out over the mattress. "I told
Zack you'd be mad," Tony informed her, hopping
back and forth from one bare foot to the other as he

pulled the sheet up under the pillow. "But Heather really needed that cookie, Mom. Her stomach was growling real loud."

"Then Heather should have finished her supper," Samantha replied smoothly.

As always, Zack was quick to jump to his little sister's defense. "That soup was yucky."

Tony was much too diplomatic to agree with that uncomplimentary assessment of his mother's cooking, but Samantha saw the long-suffering look on his face as he crawled back into bed. To be honest she thought the soup was pretty yucky herself. Boiled carrots and canned peas in beef broth didn't make for very tasty or rib-sticking fare, but she needed to stretch what little meat they had left for as long as possible, because who knew how long the snow would keep up. She really couldn't blame the kids for sneaking food into bed with them, even if oatmeal cookies and peppermint candy were less-than-nutritious choices.

Besieged by guilt, Samantha opened the jar of peanut butter and spread a generous, high-protein portion on three slices of bread. As she handed them out to her wide-eyed children, she said, "We may not have much money, but none of you ever has to go to bed hungry. Is that understood?"

The question earned her three nods and Zack's request for a glass of milk. Samantha tripled his order and sat down on the mattress to watch as every drop was consumed. "Now go to sleep," she ordered firmly, after gathering up the empty glasses and retucking the quilts.

Heather's eyelids were drooping, and Tony was beginning to look drowsy, but Zack still seemed wide-awake. She didn't know if it would be better to wait until they were all sleeping before she went out to the barn, or if she should tell them she was going and let them worry about her until she got back, just as she was going to worry about leaving them alone in the house.

As if he could read her mind, Zack said, "Mom, you'd better go. We can't lose Maizie or her baby. I'll stay up till you get back in the house, so if Maizie has trouble calving, you can come get me. I can help."

A lump formed in Samantha's throat as she listened to the offer of a boy far too young to be saddled with adult responsibilities, and she screamed silent curses at the man who had forced such a burden on his own son. Right after the divorce hearing, Brad, her philandering ex-husband, had simply packed up and disappeared, and she'd yet to receive her first child-support payment. Since Samantha couldn't afford to hire an investigator to track him down, there was a good possibility that Brad would never meet his obligations. For him, she called forth damnation, but for his courageous child, she brought forth her most radiant smile and reached down to tousle his blond curls.

"I know I can always count on your help, Zack, but you don't need to stay up. Maizie won't have trouble giving birth," she said, trying to reassure herself as much as her son. "She's delivered lots of calves, and this one will come just as easily as all her other ones. I just want to make sure it's warm and dry enough in the barn for the new baby. I shouldn't be gone very long."

"Okay," Zack said, sounding relieved.

Samantha bent down and kissed his cheek. "Sleep tight."

"Be careful, Mom," Zack advised, striving hard to control the quaver in his voice as he allowed himself to be tucked in for the third time. "That wind sounds kind of creepy."

Determined that he wouldn't sense a similar fear in herself, Samantha scoffed, "It's just a blustery old howler, Zack. It'll blow itself out by morning."

Though her words seemed to soothe him, Samantha wasn't certain until she took a last check before going outside. Zack was sound asleep. Exhausted herself, Samantha prayed that Maizie would prove her right and have an easy delivery. It had been years since she'd helped at a birthing, and she wasn't sure she could remember what to do.

As she pushed open the front door, the wind tore at her bulky coat and almost snatched her tousle cap from her head. It was nearly impossible to see. At least she'd had enough forethought to tie a rope between the barn and the house before the storm had gained full force. She was going to need it. Since she was only slightly more than five feet tall, she sank up to her knees in snow with every step. Progress was slow, but by clinging to the rope with both hands, she managed to pull herself forward step by step.

Luckily the wind had swept the area in front of the barn door clean, rather than depositing a drift that she would have had to dig out to gain entry. It was a struggle to close the door after herself, but she didn't mind the exertion. Holding on to the rope while shoveling snow would have been twice as hard.

She was also relieved to discover that even though it was freezing outside, the interior of the barn was reasonably warm. Like the house, the barn's roof needed to be replaced, but until the snow began to melt, the interior would stay relatively dry. Moving to the first stall, Samantha saw that another of her major worries was over. Maizie had already delivered, and mother and calf appeared to be doing just fine.

After taking a closer look, she felt free to move on to the next stall, which housed her two sickly heifers. Although they didn't look any better, neither did they seem any worse. Still, as Samantha leaned over to pet one on the head, the animal showed little interest, and the hay she'd pitched into the stall earlier remained uneaten. If the animals stayed off their feed like this and lost much more weight, they wouldn't be worth what she'd paid for them.

However, there was nothing more she could do for them tonight. Samantha was just starting for the door when she heard the soft whinny of a horse. Since she didn't own any horses, the sound stopped her in her tracks. To her astonishment, as she peered down the aisle to the last stall, she saw a huge, roan stallion.

At first she thought she was seeing things, but when she turned on the light at the back of the barn, the horse was still there. And he wasn't her only unexpected guest, she realized a few moments later as she stepped up on the bottom rail of the rear stall to stroke the stallion's muzzle. In the back corner was a man, wearing nothing but a horse blanket and sleeping on a pile of straw!

He was curled up in the fetal position, but she could still tell that he was a big man. His exposed right shoulder was broad and muscular, and even in sleep, the biceps of his upper arm was large and imposing. So were the muscles of his lower calves that the blanket didn't stretch far enough to cover. And his face was a perfect match for his powerful body, with features as rugged as the rest of him and skin bronzed by years of exposure to the sun.

His brown hair was blunt cut and streaked with auburn highlights that gleamed like burnished copper in the barn light. Long sideburns accentuated his high cheekbones and the stubborn jut of his square jaw. The only feminine thing about him were the supremely long and curly brown lashes closed over what Samantha knew were a pair of deep-set brown eyes.

It had taken her only a second to recognize him. Asleep or awake, with or without clothes, he was none other than Steven Armstrong, owner of the Triple A Ranch, one of the largest spreads in Montana. He was also corporate chief of Armstrong Enterprises, a conglomerate of concerns ranging from copper mining to oil. As difficult as it was to believe, the near-naked man huddled up on a pile of hay in her ramshackle barn was the head of a powerful family dynasty that dated back over a century.

Until she'd found a land deed among a pile of her father's old papers, Samantha had assumed that the Armstrongs had finally convinced him to sell out these acres that bordered the eastern edge of their vast holdings. Samantha knew that they'd been after the property for years and was surprised to discover that her father had somehow managed to hang on to it even though she'd heard his views on the subject many times as she was growing up. If Caleb Todd had anything to say about it, the rich wouldn't be getting any richer off him. Although he'd eventually lost interest in everything except the inside of a whiskey bottle, he'd apparently never compromised on that stance.

When it came to her father, Samantha had very little to feel proud about, but at least he'd accomplished one worthwhile thing in his life, even if it was owing to his sheer mean-minded stubbornness. No matter what had prompted him to hold out, the result was that she, not the Armstrongs, still owned this small section of land. As she glared down at the first-born son of that all-powerful family, a glimmer of satisfaction shone in her eyes.

The last time she'd seen Steven Armstrong, she'd been a child of ten, and he'd been in his early twenties, but she'd never forgotten his arrogant face or what he'd said to her that day. She'd been out hunting crawdads, squishing her bare toes in the soft mud on the banks of Calico Creek, when two men had ridden up to water their horses. Gazing down at her from atop an animal much like the one he rode now, he'd commented to the man with him, "It's that ornery old squatter's kid. She's a cute little mite now, but you know what happens to her kind. She'll likely have at least three kids hanging on her skirts by the time she's twenty."

His companion had been many years older and less willing to condemn. He'd also given Samantha credit for being able to hear, while Steven had looked at her as if she were not only disgustingly filthy, but deaf and dumb, as well. "Old Caleb's got her in school, and Miz Leslie says she's smart as a whip," the older man had commented. "No matter what you think of her pa, this lil gal just might make something of herself."

Steven Armstrong had scoffed, "Fat chance. If her old man keeps on drinkin' like he does, she'll be pickin' up guys at the Blue Wrangler before she's too much older. That beer hall already serves as her second home."

"The way I've heard it, the same could be said for you. I understand you've got a real hankering for cute, blond waitresses, and this little gal has the makings to be a real looker. Who knows? If you wait a few more years and mosey on into the place, you just might like what you see."

"I may have a taste for blondes, but I prefer my women clean and sober. Look at that dirty ring around her neck. The kid hasn't seen the inside of a bathtub in months, and it wouldn't surprise me if her pa hasn't already given her a taste for beer." Dark eyes flashing with ire, he'd continued, "Somebody should report him and have her taken away."

The older man had reproved, "I realize you've got your dander up because Caleb just turned down another very generous offer, but that doesn't make him a bad father. Underneath all that mud, she looks plenty healthy to me."

"Like I said, just give her a couple more years."

Samantha hadn't been old enough to comprehend the full import of Steven's predictions, but she'd understood his contemptuous tone and read the pity in his intense brown eyes as they'd surveyed her patched jeans, wrinkled shirt and mud-splotched face. Even back then she couldn't stand to be pitied, and she'd proved it by picking up a stone and pitching it at his head. She'd scampered away out of sight before he'd regained control of his rearing horse, but she could still recall the violent threats he'd hurled after her.

As the years passed, that incident had returned to haunt her more times than she would like to count, and Samantha hated the fact that this man's assessment of her had come so close to the truth. Though she'd never developed a taste for beer, she *had* met Brad at the Blue Wrangler and been married by seventeen. At least that arrogant, know-it-all Armstrong had been wrong about the number of kids she would have by the age of twenty. She'd managed to put off giving birth to her third child until she was twenty-one.

Samantha wasn't aware of the hostility shimmering in her large blue eyes as she stared over the rail, but it was the first thing Steven noticed when he opened his. The next thing he observed was a flawless complexion, near-perfect features and hair that glistened like spun gold. Her body was hidden inside bulky winter clothes, but if it was anything like that face, she was one beautiful woman.

It wasn't easy, but somehow Steven managed to get to his feet without dropping the blanket that hid his nakedness from her sight. He'd never been that modest, but something about the way this woman was staring at him, as if she could see right through the tattered blanket to his bare skin and didn't like what she saw, made him highly uncomfortable. Even more disconcerting was the fact that she didn't try to hide her gratification as she scrutinized the dull red flush creeping up his neck and the shivers that wracked his body as a cold draft whisked up beneath the blanket and over his exposed backside.

Hoping to ease the mounting tension between them, Steven spoke in the slow drawl that had charmed countless other women. "I'm real sorry for imposing on your hospitality like this, ma'am, but when Challenger and I stumbled in here this afternoon, we weren't up to asking for an invite."

Even though she knew quite well that the man had been seeking protection from the storm, and that both he and his horse might have died if they hadn't reached the shelter of her barn, Samantha felt a spiteful lack of sympathy for his recent ordeal. It was gratifying to know that a mighty Armstrong could suffer from the cold just like any other lesser mortal and flush with embarrassment when caught with his pants down. "Which makes you a trespasser," she observed shortly.

Taken aback by the accusation, Steven's mouth dropped open, but he made no move to step closer to the rail. The woman was obviously a bit fearful at finding a strange man asleep in the barn, and he didn't want to add to her uneasiness. Her inhospitable attitude told him that she was probably living alone out here, so he could understand why she would be wary.

As for his being a trespasser, the mere mention of his name would take care of that ridiculous charge. "The name's Armstrong. Steven Armstrong. I'm sure you've heard of it."

Without batting an eyelash, Samantha lied, "No, why should I?"

*Because you're squatting on my land, that's why,* Steven wanted to shout, but he doubted anyone could fake such a blank look. At the same time, he decided that any dispute about rightful ownership could wait until later. When he'd first arrived, he'd been far too numb, cold and exhausted to put two and two together and realize that an occupied barn meant an occupied house. Now that he had, he concluded that the house would be a much warmer place to conduct their conversation.

"In this part of the country, most people have heard of me or my family," he stated truthfully as he walked over to the hay bale where he'd spread out his wet clothes. They weren't close to dry, but he couldn't very well go outside in a near gale-force wind wearing nothing but this threadbare blanket.

"Is that so." Samantha kept her expression blank, refusing to give him the satisfaction of recognizing his supposedly revered name. The passing years had done nothing to lessen his colossal arrogance and conceit, but if he expected her to bow down before his greatness, he could wait forever.

"I'm the owner of the Triple A Ranch," he elaborated helpfully, still hoping to attain her acknowledgment that he was her absentee landlord. Once she realized who he was, he was sure that she would offer to let him warm up in the house. In exchange for the amount of time she'd lived here rent free, she owed him at least that much.

"Good for you."

So much for that hope, Steven thought as he fumbled to pull on his wet jeans without dropping the blanket. Giving up on his first unproductive tack, he tried another. "So I'm your closest neighbor," he informed her, wincing as he drew a sodden wool sock over his freezing right foot. The left sock was just as soggy, and neither foot appreciated being thrust into stiff leather boots. Unable to stomach the thought of replacing his wet shirt and jacket, he ripped a small hole in the blanket into a larger one and pulled it over his head. Draping it over his chest serape fashion, he used his belt to secure it around his middle.

Since the woman watching him seemed reluctant to follow simple logic, he gave her a little push. "And since I've never been this cold in my life, I'd consider it right neighborly of you to invite me into your warm house for some dry clothes, a nice hot cup of coffee and the use of a phone."

"My clothes wouldn't fit you, and I don't have a phone," Samantha stated uncharitably, then felt a twinge of guilt when she saw him shiver. "But I suppose I could make you some coffee if I have any left."

"Gee, thanks," Steven bit out, no longer hiding how he felt about her less-than-generous attitude.

Samantha flushed, suddenly ashamed of how niggardly she was behaving. She would treat a stray dog better than she was treating this man. Then again, dogs were usually much nicer than most people, especially men, and they often deserved better treatment.

As soon as he'd jammed his cold fingers into his stiff gloves, Steven climbed over the rail, but the woman standing beside him didn't seem inclined to let him move past her down the aisle. She was awfully short, he noted, but she wasn't the least bit intimidated by the imposing difference in their heights. According to her hostile expression, she still wasn't too sure that she should allow him into her house and was prepared to take him on physically if it became necessary.

Steven thought better of laughing. "Please, lady, I swear I'm harmless," he promised through chattering teeth. "I'll be out of your hair as soon as I can."

After considering his words for several long seconds, she turned her back on him and walked swiftly up the aisle, not waiting to see if he followed. Fearing she might still change her mind, Steven was right on her heels.

"I've got a rope tied to the house," she called back over her shoulder as she heaved open the barn door. "It's about a foot to the left and waist high."

Since her waist and his were at two vastly different heights, it took Steven a few moments to locate it. By the time he did, his ungracious hostess had disappeared into the thick curtain of swirling snow. Since he wouldn't have put it past her to cut the other end once she reached it and leave him floundering outside in the blizzard, he hurried to catch up with her. Unfortunately he was moving too fast to stop when she did, and the force of contact sent them both sprawling forward into a deep drift.

"For cripes sakes, of all the idiotic . . ." Samantha spat out a mouthful of snow and tried to squirm out from under his considerable weight, but she couldn't move. "Get off me, you big, clumsy lummox!"

With malice of forethought, Steven took more time than necessary to comply with her order. He could tell that beneath her bulky clothes, the body pinned under him was a lightweight, but its owner had a heavyweight mouth. He was used to a certain amount of deference from the female of the species, and no woman had ever spoken to him in such a contemptuous tone or questioned his intelligence. Running into her had been an accident, but Steven made sure she got a little snow down her stiff neck before he helped her back to her feet. "Are you okay?" he inquired with mock concern.

"No thanks to you," Samantha huffed, shivering in her boots as a trickle of cold water ran down her spine and another one worked its way between her breasts. "Watch where you're going from now on, would you? I'd like to make it back to the house in one piece."

Steven had a vengeful urge to lift the rope up out of her reach, but when he saw the snow sticking to her soft, sooty eyelashes and wispy blond bangs, he resisted it. She was awfully small, and he'd been taught not to pick on somebody who wasn't his own size. "Sorry about that," he apologized. "I lost sight of you there for a minute, and I guess I got a little panicky."

As she regained her hold on the rope, Samantha shot him a disbelieving look, which Steven didn't see any better than she saw his unrepentant grin. A burst of angry wind stirred up a flurry of icy flakes and hurled them at their faces. Samantha was thrown off balance, but Steven grabbed her collar and saved her from falling down again.

Feeling like a tiny, helpless kitten held up by the scruff of her neck, Samantha groped for a better hold on the rope. The instant she had it, she began to struggle out of his firm grip, but he was slow to release her.

"Let go of me!"

"You're so welcome," Steven bit out sarcastically, fighting back another grin as he removed his helping hand.

"C'mon," Samantha shouted over the rising wind. "If we don't get moving, we're going to freeze to death out here."

"I'm right behind you," Steven shouted back.

"How reassuring," Samantha grumbled under her breath as, hand over hand, she worked her way toward the house.

# Two

Dressed in a pink brushed-flannel bathrobe that barely came down to his knees and a pair of red wool socks that could only be stretched to cover his ankles, Steven felt like a fool because he looked like one. Tossing a longing gaze at the wet shirt, socks, underwear and jeans that were hung on a clothesline stretched over the furnace grate in the kitchen floor, he darted out from behind the bedroom curtain. Two fast, giant strides and he slid quickly into his seat at the round oak table. With any luck, he thought, no one had witnessed his embarrassed dash for the table, but when he looked up, he saw that luck was a lady with mocking blue eyes.

"Thanks for the coffee," he mumbled, using one hand to hold the edges of the feminine robe together over his chest and the other to lift the steaming mug to his lips. "And for the...eh...dry clothes. I don't think I woke any of your kids when I changed."

"Good," Samantha replied, turning back to the stove to hide her amused smile. It was hard not to laugh at his ridiculous appearance, and the effort made her voice sound stiff. "It took me a long time to get them settled down. I wouldn't appreciate going through that routine twice in one night."

Since he was doing his best to be polite and had complied with her order not to make much noise when he changed, Steven didn't appreciate being spoken to in the tones of a strict schoolmarm who was amazed to hear that one of her least capable students could follow a simple instruction. In looks and size, she was the one lacking in maturity, yet she didn't seem to notice that at thirty-six, he had to be her senior by at least ten years. Before too much more time had passed, he intended to get that point across, which was going to be easier said than done considering his schoolboy reaction whenever she glanced at him.

As soon as they'd reached the house and she'd removed her coat and hat, he'd realized that she was even better looking than he'd first thought and even more tiny. She reminded him of a small yellow warbler with delicate bones, and wings poised for instant flight at the slightest sign of danger. She had a musical lilt to her voice that couldn't be hidden even though she'd yet to warble anything nice, and like the colorful songbird, she also had a surprisingly full breast for her size.

Steven found himself wanting to coax her fear of him away. Unused to treading lightly with a woman, it was a new and unsettling experience for him. He knew he was a big man, but he'd never had a woman shy away from him if he came anywhere near her. Her skittish reaction to him made him feel clumsy and grated on his nerves—most women considered him a real sweet guy.

"I hope you plan to join me in a cup," he tried, striving for a friendly tone. "You must be just as cold as I am." He reached for the sugar bowl, then quickly changed his mind when his bathrobe fell open all the way down to his navel. Afraid of how she might react to the sight of his bare chest, he made a frantic grab for the gaping material and nearly knocked over both the sugar bowl and his coffee in the process.

As she poured herself a cup, Samantha struggled to contain her amusement. She hadn't liked the thought of sharing company, let alone anything else, with an Armstrong, but she wouldn't have missed this opportunity for the world. Knocked off his high horse, Steven Armstrong didn't seem half as large and intimidating as he had when she was a child.

Considering their past acquaintance, she was complimented by his nervousness around her. A few years back, the shoe had definitely been on the other foot, and she couldn't help but enjoy the feeling that she was getting some of her own back. Though she knew he didn't think so, she thought he looked quite fetching in a ruffled satin collar and bright pink flannel flowers. As she took the chair across from him, she decided that the pink robe was a perfect match for the becoming color in his cheeks and enhanced the marvelous color of his dark eyes.

Her own eyes widened with shock as she realized what she was feeling. After all these years, she was physically attracted to Steven Armstrong! How could this be? She immediately experienced an odd, panicky sensation in the pit of her stomach, and her brain switched into overdrive.

Okay, she assured herself. Her stupid body might be attracted to him, but she could fix that problem. If the way to a man's heart was through his stomach, she would soon see the last of this one. "If you're hungry," she offered, "I could heat up some of the soup we had for supper. There's plenty left."

Avoiding the intense gaze that lingered rudely on his ridiculous getup, Steven admitted, "I haven't eaten since breakfast. I'll appreciate anything you're kind enough to offer."

Samantha sucked in her lower lip to hide a telltale smile. After taking a few sips of her coffee, she got up and returned to the stove. She'd intended to toss out the congealed liquid that remained in the kettle, but he needn't know that. "This will only take a few minutes to heat up."

Steven nodded. "Thanks, Mrs....?"

"Samantha, Samantha Charles."

Steven frowned as the woman turned her back on him. She'd provided her name, but he still didn't know her marital status, and the more time he spent with her the more anxious he was to find out. He'd always had a weakness for blondes, and this one might be small, but she was definitely a keeper. Beyond that, her standoffish attitude challenged him on a level he'd never experienced before. After the number of women he'd associated with over the years, new experiences were a novelty.

He'd always had a way with women, but with her, none of his past techniques seemed to work. His winning smile didn't melt the ice in her gaze. A polite manner didn't soften the stiffness around her beguiling mouth, and though he'd done his best to behave in a nonthreatening manner, she was still wary. He couldn't understand it, and that made him all the more determined to change it.

He was equally determined to find out how she'd come upon this isolated, run-down old place and why in the devil she'd chosen to move in. The last time he'd been inside old Caleb's cabin, it had been empty of anything but field mice and spiders. Most women would have taken one look and run off in the other direction. This one had not only stayed on, but worked hard to fix the place up.

The house was furnished sparsely, but everything was scrupulously clean. Every broken windowpane had been replaced and the windows covered by pretty handmade curtains. The walls had been patched and repainted, the woodwork sanded and revarnished and the weak floorboards repaired. As hard as it was for Steven to believe, Samantha Charles had apparently been here for quite some time, maybe even months.

Steven found it difficult to swallow that she'd done all this work by herself, but there was no evidence to the contrary. Although the three small children asleep behind the curtain must have a father, there was no sign of a man in residence. A quick glance around the cramped room had disclosed a double bed for the children and a single bed nearby. There were only female toiletries on the dresser, and the open closet door had revealed nothing but women's and children's clothes.

Steven doubted he would be wearing her bathrobe if Samantha Charles had anything better suited for his sex. So what had become of Mr. Charles? Steven wondered. Was Samantha a divorced woman surviving on minimal child support? Or worse, had she been left a penniless widow? In either case, if she really was destitute, how could he kick her and her three young children out of their home? Even if they had no legal right to be living here, he wouldn't have the heart to ask them to move.

Yet living here wasn't safe, Steven thought as he listened to the mounting death throes of an ancient furnace. Although the woman had done her best to make the place habitable, the living conditions were still substandard. The walls were too thin, the plumbing primitive, and if the blinking lights were any indication, the electrical wiring was haphazard at best. The threat of fire was a definite danger, and according to the sounds coming from the furnace, it wouldn't be long before it would be just as cold inside the house as out. Somehow or another he was going to have to convince her to move, but she was so defensive already, he didn't dare broach the subject.

"I went a bit overboard with the carrots," Samantha apologized as she returned to the table a few minutes later, carrying a bowl of hot soup. "But I was short on potatoes, and in this weather I couldn't get to town."

Steven hated carrots, but since this was the first un-begrudging offer she'd made to him, he didn't admit it. "Looks good," he complimented as he dipped his spoon into the large bowl she set down before him. Unfortunately he couldn't hide his reaction to the gruesome taste and made a face.

"Too hot?" Samantha asked, knowing very well that a burned tongue wasn't his problem.

"A bit." Steven nodded, grateful for any excuse she cared to offer him.

Samantha scraped back her chair. "I'll get you a glass of cold water, and you can add enough to get it to the right temperature."

"That's okay," Steven negated swiftly. If the soup got any weaker, it would taste even more like dirty water. The soggy carrots and peas already reminded him of the kind of waste that floated in the sink before he turned on the garbage disposal. "Once I finish my coffee, it should be cooled off just fine."

In the meantime maybe he could figure out a way to rid himself of the noxious liquid without swallowing it or offending her. Unfortunately that opportunity never presented itself. Samantha watched him like a hawk, and as soon as he took his last sip of coffee, she inquired, "How's that soup now?"

The eager expression on her face reminded Steven of his Aunt Polly, who arrived at the ranch each spring with a fresh batch of her home-brewed elixir. A spoonful was guaranteed to turn any man's stomach and make his eyes water. Even so, he and his younger brother, Robert, and their foreman, Conlan Fox, had managed to ingest their annual dosage without upchucking. How much harder could it be to gulp down a bowl full of beef broth, stewed carrots and an occasional pea?

Holding his breath, Steven lifted the bowl and started swallowing, telling himself to pretend he was trying to prove his manhood at a beer-guzzling contest at the Blue Wrangler. On his twenty-first birthday he'd taken on every man in the place and had lived to tell the story. If he could survive that gut-wrenching ordeal, he could surely survive this one, he decided as the lukewarm broth and decomposed vegetables slithered down his throat.

"The way you finished that off, you must really be starving," Samantha exclaimed as Steven set the empty bowl back on the table. "Let me get you some more."

Needing all his concentration to keep down what he'd already ingested, Steven could only shake his head in a helpless plea for mercy. He looked so green about the gills that Samantha took pity on him. The man had several bad points, but bad manners wasn't one of them. "You're a very polite man, Steven Armstrong, but one of these days, you might choke on those good manners. Even my own children, who love me dearly, couldn't stomach that awful soup."

Stunned by her trilling laughter as much as her teasing words, Steven's jaw fell open. Both things elated him so much that he couldn't work up any anger at her for setting him up. For the first time since he'd met her, her big blue eyes were sparkling, and a smile transformed her lovely face. As far as Steven was concerned, any price he had to pay for the delightful sight would have been well worth it.

Grinning like a lovesick calf, he asked, "Did anyone ever tell you that for such a little lady, you've got a mighty big mean streak?"

"How could I have predicted that you'd guzzle it all down like that?" Samantha asked between giggles. "Most people would have waited until I turned my back, then dumped it in that potted plant."

"What potted plant?" Steven swiveled around in his chair, groaning when, not a foot away, he spied a huge brass pot and a sickly looking growth of some kind. "Now you tell me."

"How could you miss it?"

"Beats me," Steven admitted. "By the looks of that poor thing, not too many others have."

Samantha sniffed in mock indignation. "I'll have you know that I'm considered a very good cook."

Steven chuckled, his brown eyes twinkling. "Uh-huh."

"Well, I am."

"Okay, I'll give you the chance to prove it at breakfast. I like my eggs scrambled, my bacon crisp and my orange juice freshly squeezed without pits."

It was Samantha's turn to feel her jaw drop, and her reaction had nothing to do with his audacious challenge. Once again she was aware that her unwelcome guest was a man, a very attractive man, who knew his way around women. Even knowing what she did about him, he'd managed to charm his way past her defenses and make her laugh. "Breakfast? You won't be here for breakfast!'' she burst out frantically. ''As soon as your clothes are dry, you'll have to leave.''

''The farthest I'd make it would be to the barn.''

For some stupid reason, Samantha hadn't acknowledged the obvious until this moment. Of course he would be here at breakfast and possibly much longer. Under current weather conditions, she was well and truly stuck with him. ''I couldn't expect you to stay in the barn,'' she admitted, leaving him with no doubt as to how she felt about having him in the house.

''Though you'd like to,'' he muttered curtly.

''Of course I wouldn't,'' Samantha replied. What she really wanted to do was ask him to take both his horse and himself completely off her property and stay off.

Steven didn't need her to tell him what she was thinking. Exasperated, he wondered what it was about him that made her look as if she were being forced to spend the night with Jack the Ripper. For a few minutes there, they'd been laughing and talking, and he thought he'd been making some headway with her, but now it appeared they were back to square one.

Savoring the thought of how badly she would feel once he'd proved to her that he was her landlord, he promised, ''Don't worry. I'll do my best to earn my keep while I'm here.''

Samantha looked doubtful.

''You'll see. I'm a handy guy to have around in a snowstorm,'' he insisted.

''Is that so?''

Refusing to lose his temper, Steven declared evenly, "To get through tomorrow, you're going to need a man, and as far as I can tell, you don't have one."

Bristling at his arrogance, Samantha snapped, "I don't have one because I don't want one!"

Eyeing her in a wicked way that made her entire body feel warm, Steven drawled, "Wanting a man and needing him are two different things."

"Let me assure you, Mr. Armstrong. Where you're concerned, neither term applies."

His dark eyes glittered with amusement and something far more dangerous. He smiled slowly, and it changed him, changed everything. Even dressed in a woman's robe, he was devastatingly male, and that knowing smile told her he was conscious of her awareness. "You might not like admitting it, Miss Charles, but you *do* need me."

"Mrs. Charles!"

With a mocking lift of one brow, he inquired, "Hung on to the title, but not the man?"

"The man wasn't worth hanging on to."

Unfortunately the bitter words didn't foster the desired response. Samantha had hoped that her tone implied a blanket condemnation of the entire male sex, but Steven looked more pleased than insulted by her admission. "So you're divorced?"

"Not that it's any of your business."

Still smiling that infuriating smile, Steven said, "But it *does* confirm that you need my help."

"For what?"

"To water and feed your stock for one thing," Steven countered. "By morning, someone's going to have to dig a path out to the barn, and you'll have to admit, I've got a bit more brawn than you do. If it doesn't stop snowing soon, the drifts will be over your head. It could take you days to get back out there."

"I'd manage," Samantha replied tartly, but since they both knew there was no way she could turn him out in weather like this, she gave in to the inevitable. Resigned to her miserable fate, she got up from the table, walked to the closet and pulled down a pillow and a heavy quilt from the top shelf.

"You can sleep on the couch," she declared curtly, marching into the living area and dumping the bedding on the worn cushions.

"Thank you, that will be fine."

"And you can just leave those dishes. I'll do them in the morning."

"All right," Steven said, glad he didn't have to admit that doing the dishes had never entered his mind. He'd already done quite a good job of putting her off, and he was sure that chauvinistic disclosure would have added even more distance. He was about to suggest that they share a last cup of coffee in the hopes he would be able to recover some lost ground, but Samantha had other ideas.

"Then I'll see you in the morning," she tossed over her shoulder and disappeared behind the bedroom curtain before he could get another word out of his mouth.

Steven frowned at the curtain for several seconds, shook his head in frustration, then got up from the table to complete the chores Samantha would've done if she hadn't been so all-fired anxious to get away from him. He checked the lock on the front door, made sure all the burners were turned off on the kitchen stove and switched off the lights. He stubbed his toe on his way to the couch, almost knocking over the wooden chair in the process, and grunted loudly in pain, but his reluctant hostess didn't make any inquiries concerning his welfare. Either she didn't hear him, or she didn't care that he might have injured himself.

As he covered himself with the blanket and tried to find a comfortable position on the short couch, Steven feared it was the latter.

Not since her mother had been alive had Samantha awoke in the morning to the smell of frying bacon and freshly brewed coffee. She was staring at the same faded blue wallpaper that had greeted her back then, and for a few seconds, she almost believed that by some miracle, she was five years old again. The high-pitched laughter of three other children confirmed her foolish indulgence in that flight of fancy, and the rattle of pots and pans brought her to full wakefulness.

One glance at the clock and Samantha shot out of bed. It was half past eight! Ever since she'd moved out to the ranch, she'd been up by six to start chores. So what made this morning any different?

Not wishing to delve too closely into the possible answers to that question, Samantha blotted it out of her mind and hurriedly pulled on a pair of jeans and a long-sleeved flannel shirt. If she could believe her ears, the millionaire owner of one of the largest ranches in Montana was standing in her humble kitchen and making breakfast for her children. This was something she really had to see.

When Samantha stepped out from around the curtain, the reality of the scene before her was even more astounding than the one she'd imagined. Steven Armstrong had looked absolutely ridiculous in her pink flannel robe, but he appeared perfectly at ease wearing jeans, his well-worn shirt and one of her best frilly aprons. To the wide-eyed delight of his young audience, he was flipping pancakes up in the air and catching them in a heavy cast-iron skillet with the expertise of a fry cook at a lumber camp.

He was facing the stove and wasn't aware of Samantha's presence as he boasted, "Nothing to it, guys. It's all in the wrist. Ready?"

"Ready!" three children chorused back to him.

"Then, heads up!" he warned, wielding a large spatula like a tennis racket. The children obediently ducked as a golden-brown flapjack sailed through the air and landed on the platter in the center of the kitchen table. This feat was followed by a round of enthusiastic clapping from the kids, a shocked gasp from their mother and a welcoming smile from the dexterous chef.

"Good morning," Steven greeted before turning back to the stove. "I know you were hoping to show me what a great cook you are this morning, but the kids and I got too hungry to wait any longer for you to wake up. Hope you like pancakes, Samantha. I think I made the batter kind of heavy, but this was the best I could do."

"I only got a glimpse of the one that just flew over my daughter's head, but it looked light enough to me," Samantha replied as she took her seat at the head of the table. She wasn't sure if she should applaud him for providing such enjoyable early-morning entertainment or chastise him for attempting such a dangerous stunt. She decided that it was her duty as a mother to mention the possible consequences of his actions. "I'm glad everyone managed to get out of the way before somebody got burned."

According to the succession of flying flour saucers that followed her comment, the man wasn't greatly concerned about inflicting bodily harm. To his credit, a warning was shouted before each takeoff, but it was hardly necessary. Missing all onlookers, every disk made a precision landing on the platter.

"I never miss," Steven announced grandly, once the platter was stacked high. "And like I said, I owe it all to my great teacher, Paul."

As he placed a plate of bacon down on the table and took the seat opposite hers, Samantha opened her mouth to ask him Paul who, but Zack answered her question before she could voice it. "Cuz Paul Bunyan had to cook a zillion flapjacks a day for the blue ox," he informed her. "Babe had a powerful likin' for 'em."

"And since he was too big to sit down at the table," Tony picked up on the story, "Paul had to flip them all the way out to the pasture."

"Cross two, way-big mountains," Heather added enthusiastically.

"At first, Steven's arm got real tuckered, and he couldn't even get one over the first mountain," Zack said. "But then Paul Bunyan taught him some fancy wrist action, and now he can flip flapjacks clean over the Rockies."

"So to me, a couple of feet is mere child's play," Steven concluded smugly, showing off the flexibility in his right wrist.

"I see," Samantha mumbled, fighting down laughter and the sudden urge she had to cry. After the age of six, she'd done without tall tales and fairy stories and had forgotten all the enchanting yarns her mother had once told her. Because she'd forgotten, she hadn't thought to pass them on to her own children. Looking at their animated faces, she realized how very remiss she'd been.

Yesterday she'd been angrily blaming her ex-husband for laying a heavy burden of responsibility on shoulders too young to carry the load, but wasn't she guilty of an equally unfair crime? After dealing so long with the harsh realities of life, she'd neglected to teach her children what fun could be had escaping into a world of pure fantasy. Children had the right to explore the farthest reaches of their imaginations, yet she'd unwittingly limited her own offspring to the here and the now.

She found it even more upsetting that of all people, Steven Armstrong was the one who'd provided them with this kind of enjoyment, a man she'd despised for almost as long as she'd done without castles and kings and giant lumberjacks who could flip flapjacks over way-big mountains. Refusing to be outdone by the likes of him, Samantha searched the seldom-used paths of her childhood memory, and to her amazement found just the right thing.

She tasted a bite of pancake and smiled up at Steven. "Paul Bunyan taught you well, Mr. Armstrong, but not as well as my teacher taught me. You see, Paul was a much better pancake eater than he was a pancake maker, and I was taught by the woman who knew that better than anybody—his wife, Carrie."

Three incredulous pairs of blue eyes turned in her direction. "Really, Mom?" Tony asked, sitting up straighter in his chair. "Is that why your pancakes taste so good?"

Casting a triumphant glance at Steven, Samantha elaborated on her story. "Yes, sirree, Carrie was a magnificent cook and the perfect wife for a logger. She could split rails with no head on her ax handle and could split five thousand in a single day. She was a size to match Paul, too. It took thirteen blankets to make her a skirt and the sail of a full-rigged ship to make her undergarments. She needed an extra big moose hide to fit just one foot, yet she could run faster than anything."

"That's no proof that she could cook," Steven pointed out, grinning at the rapt expressions on the children's faces. "Is it, guys?"

"If she taught my mom, she hadda been great," Tony declared loyally.

"Just not soup," Heather clarified softly.

"I'll say," Steven agreed, gratified when Samantha laughed.

"Well, to be honest, chicken was Carrie's specialty," Samantha admitted, warming to her story. "She generally used to clean two and a half dozen every night to get ready for breakfast in the morning. But when she went out to the logging camp, Paul had to ship in a few hundred dozen more while she was there. Otherwise his crew would up and stop work, just to smell the ones Carrie was cooking for him."

Tony nodded his head at Steven. "Mom's chicken is purty special, mister."

Steven smiled at the small boy. "I'd say her chicken isn't the only thing that's special about her."

Samantha flushed at the compliment, but the children didn't give her much time to savor it. They wanted to hear all about her cooking lessons with Paul Bunyan's wife, and she was very happy to tell them.

# Three

As he sat back and listened to Samantha regale her children with the nonsensical exploits of one Carrie McIntie Bunyan, Steven found that he was enjoying himself more than he had in a long while. Sitting down to breakfast in a minuscule kitchen with three laughing children and their lovely mother was much more pleasant than taking his meals alone at a table large enough to seat twelve. The contentment he felt this morning was confirmation of his problem.

It wasn't so much that he was sick of retiring to his study night after night with a stack of paperwork. Armstrong Enterprises had kept him extremely busy of late, but he wasn't overwhelmed by additional work. And it wasn't that he'd lost interest in playing poker with the hired hands, or that he was bored with the wild and woolly entertainment to be found at the

Blue Wrangler bar. No, the simple fact of the matter was, he was just plain lonely.

Up until nine months ago, he and his younger brother, Rob, and their foreman, Conlan Fox, had all shared the big house and everything else that went on at the Triple A Ranch. For years the three of them had worked together like a well-oiled machine. With a degree in law, Steven was most qualified to handle corporation business. Conlan was in charge of ranch operations, and since he was a vet, Rob made all decisions concerning the stock.

But with Conlan's marriage to their long-lost fifth cousin, Kerry Armstrong, all that had changed. Con had turned in his resignation as foreman so he and Kerry could start their own place. Then, after purchasing Kerry's old home, Laurel Glen, Rob had packed up and left for Connecticut, intent on making the ancestral Armstrong estate into the successful thoroughbred breeding farm it had been in years past. Suddenly Steven not only found himself in sole charge of every facet of the family business, but living alone in a twenty-room house.

He could deal with the additional responsibilities thrust upon him, but to his amazement, he wasn't dealing very well with his loneliness. Recently it had occurred to him that what he'd worked so hard to build up and whatever building was to be done in the future wouldn't affect anybody besides him very much.

In the months since their departure, Steven had come to the realization that none of the people closest to him would be coming back for anything more than an occasional visit. Oh, Rob had flown back for Christmas, and Conlan and Kerry had stayed over for a few days during the holidays, but that had been that. For the rest of the winter, he'd been alone with the snow and the cold and the unending solitude. Not even the knowledge that spring was coming had helped alleviate his feelings of isolation. Whatever the season, he was on his own.

Steven shook his head at the unusual circumstances that had relieved him of his melancholy mood. If not for a marauding pack of wolves and a freak blizzard, he would be feeling just as sorry for himself today as he had been yesterday. Instead he was filling himself up on flapjacks and maple syrup, listening to the tall tales of a beautiful storyteller and enjoying the delighted laughter of her three young children. Somebody up there obviously had a very unique sense of humor.

"Why so surprised? Men aren't the only bigger-than-life characters represented in American folklore."

The brusque question brought Steven out of his reverie. "Huh?"

"For every Wild Bill Hickok, there's an Annie Oakley," Samantha persisted heatedly. "And just where would Hiawatha be without his Minnehaha?"

Astonished by this unexpected attack of feminist ire, Steven came back meekly, "Over his head in deep-sea waters?"

"Exactly," Samantha declared tartly before realizing that Steven wasn't arguing with her. So if he wasn't taken aback by Carrie Bunyan's contribution to

American legend, why had he been shaking his head like that when she'd finished telling the story?

Steven chuckled at the confused look on her face. "I wasn't casting aspersions on your female heroine, Samantha. To tell you the truth, I had other things on my mind, so I was only listening with half an ear."

"Oh," Samantha said, but then her hackles rose again as she grasped the latter part of his sentence. "Sorry if I was boring you."

Although the last time he'd shaken his head had earned him a sarcastic speech, he couldn't help himself from doing it again. He'd never met a more prickly woman in his life. "I'm not bored," he promised as his eyes wandered appreciatively over her delicate features. "In fact, I don't see how any man could possibly be bored around you."

Samantha's eyes widened at the compliment. So did Steven's. She felt his gaze on her like warm fingers, tracing the soft curve of her cheek, then lower and lower yet until Samantha stopped breathing for fear of what those caressing eyes would see.

There it was again! A feeling of desire so strong it took her breath away. For the first time since her divorce, she was experiencing the involuntary physical response of a woman who was strongly attracted to a man. Her entire body burned, and she could feel her nipples harden beneath her flannel shirt.

Steven Armstrong was the last man she would ever want to inspire these kind of sensations in her, and the knowledge that he did shocked her out of her momentary paralysis. In a no-nonsense voice, she addressed the children. "We'd best get these dishes done so we can get out to the barn. The stock needs feeding."

"Did Maizie have her baby?" Tony asked as he hopped off his chair to carry his dirty dishes to the sink.

"Yes, she did," Samantha confirmed, as she followed him to the sink with her own dirty dishes. "She had a big bull calf."

"We gonna raise him or sell him for veal?" Zack asked as he gathered his and his sister's plates and silverware together.

"Sell him," Samantha replied. "The going price for veal is surprisingly high right now, and we could sure use the money. Looks like I may have to call the vet for those two sickly heifers."

"And we already paid to have 'em bred," Tony lamented, sounding much older than his age.

"So we can't afford to lose 'em," Zack declared worriedly.

Before Steven thought to lend a helping hand, Tony returned to the table to remove his dishes. Zack picked up a cloth to wipe off his sister's sticky hands, and Samantha began running water in the sink. As soon as Heather was cleaned up, Zack lifted her down from her chair, and the little girl joined her mother at the sink, climbing up on a small stepladder.

Every member of the family seemed to have an assigned task, and they went about them without complaint. Samantha washed the dishes, and Tony wiped them, except for the silverware, which was left to Heather. It was Zack's job to put the clean dishes away. As he watched the small children go about their duties and listened to the two boys' matter-of-fact talk about beef prices and breeding fees, Steven sat in stunned amazement.

They were so young—too young to concern themselves with the natural hazards and monetary risks involved in raising beef cattle. Back when he'd been their age, the only interest he'd had in the cattle was mounting a calf and pretending to be a bull rider in a rodeo. On a day like this, he and his brother Rob would have been outside digging snow forts, not worrying about the family livestock.

But then, the loss of two heifers among thousands wouldn't have been much of a financial setback to his family. It would be for this one. From what Steven could tell, their entire herd numbered about ten.

As he listened to their conversation, he realized that they had some grandiose ideas about the future. Unfortunately their plans to increase the size of their herd were totally unrealistic. For some reason Samantha was assuming that she and her children could go on living here indefinitely. Sooner or later he was going to have to tell her that he owned this house, the barn and all the surrounding land, but he just couldn't bring himself to do it quite yet. Not when she and the kids were so happy talking dreams.

"I'd be glad to take a look at those heifers for you," Steven offered as the conversation returned to that subject. "My brother's the vet, but he's taught me a few things over the years. I can recognize most cattle ailments and even treat a few of 'em myself. Maybe all that's necessary is some simple doctoring."

Both boys spoke at once: "Great!"

Steven sighed, wishing he could provoke a similar-looking smile on the face of their mother. More than anything, he would like to erase those lines of worry around her soft mouth and ease the strained expression in her blue eyes. "And if it turns out they need antibiotics, I can truck them over to my place. We've got something on hand to cure just about every disease there is, and I won't charge you to board them in our barns until they recover. That's the least I can do for a neighbor."

"Did you hear that, Mom?" Zack exclaimed.

"Thanks for the kind offer, Mr. Armstrong, but I prefer to use my own vet and pay my own way," Samantha said as she dried her wet hands on a towel. "If a person can't afford the veterinary fees, then they shouldn't be in the cattle business. I'll either make or break this ranch on my own."

Wisely Steven didn't point out that ten cows didn't exactly add up to a business, nor one section of land a cattle ranch. What she had here was a small-scale farm that she didn't even own and a future for even smaller scale profits. Even so, Steven knew she had too damned much pride to ever admit it, and pride was one trait he could readily identify with. All of the Armstrongs had plenty more than their share, himself included.

"I understand that, Samantha," he said. "But your animals need immediate treatment, and the vet won't be able to get out here until the roads are plowed. You're not exactly on the main drag, so who knows when that will be? My boys can clear a track between our two places in a couple of hours. I don't know where you're from, but in this neck of the woods, neighbors try to help each other out."

"That's all very well and good, but—"

Determined to break down her resistance, Steven interrupted her. "Okay, if you insist, we can treat the animals here, and you can pay me back for the medication. Now that the sun's shining, my foreman will be out looking for me in the helicopter. If you've got some paint, I'll make a sign that Chuck can spot from the air, and we'll be in business."

Samantha hesitated. What he said was true. Until the roads were plowed, the vet wouldn't be able to get out here. In all likelihood that wouldn't happen for several more days, and her ailing cows might be dead by then. Beyond that, if she agreed to his suggestion, Steven Armstrong would soon be out of her hair. It was the latter consideration that inspired her compliance. "We've got several gallons of old paint stored in the woodshed, but it will take some shoveling to get out there."

"Great!" Steven expounded happily, sounding so much like one of the twins that Samantha was forced to smile.

Her smile grew even wider as he stood up from the table and announced, "Get your coats, men. You heard your mother. We've got our work cut out for us this morning."

With an almost visible increase in the size of two small masculine chests, Zack and Tony responded to his command. "Yes, sir," they chorused and ran for their coats, falling all over themselves in their haste to get outside.

Samantha's lips twitched when she noticed that Steven seemed to be in just as great a rush. Sensing that all three of them might go charging out into the snow to play and forget about the job they'd set out to do, she said, "I left a snow shovel leaning up against the house next to the door. It's probably under a drift by now."

"No problem. We'll find it," Steven assured her, then questioned the boys. "Ever make a snow tunnel, boys?"

The twins shook their heads.

"My brother and I once dug a tunnel all the way from our house to the barn. Of course you need the right kind of snow," he continued knowledgeably.

"Is this the right kind?" Tony asked as he threw himself on the floor to pull on his boots.

"I'd say so," Steven granted.

"Oh, boy," Zack said enthusiastically, dragging a ski mask down over his face. "Let's go!"

As he buttoned up his sheepskin jacket, Steven outlined his game plan to the boys. "First we'll tunnel our way out to the barn so we can feed and water the stock—"

Samantha broke in to tell him that it was her responsibility to see to her stock, but he was hearing none of it. "If you want to keep things fair and square, I'll take care of the outside chores. I promised you I'd earn my keep around here, and I intend to make good on that promise."

"I don't expect you to earn your keep," Samantha said, disliking the impression he was giving her that he planned to be around for quite some time.

"It'll be my pleasure," Steven drawled politely, frustrating Samantha's desire to make an issue of it.

She almost choked on the words, but managed a weak, "Thank you."

Steven inclined his head at her, then returned his attention to the twins. "After the stock's taken care of, we'll work our way around to the shed. The sun's shining, but it's so cold that there should be a thin crust of ice on top of the snow. I'll fall right through, so I'll have to count on you two guys to make a big X with the paint. Think you can handle it?"

Without hesitation Zack declared, "No problem."

As always Tony was more cautious. After due consideration, he said, "If we're too heavy to walk on the snow, we can use snowshoes. We got an old pair in the barn."

Steven clapped him on the shoulder. "Excellent," he said, then grinned engagingly at Samantha. "We're going to work up quite an appetite out there, ma'am. Think you could have lunch waiting for us when we come back in?"

"Of course."

Brown eyes twinkling, he elaborated, "We'll need something that sticks to the ribs. Maybe some of that fried chicken you were bragging about?"

"With mash potatoes and Sunday gravy?" Zack inquired hopefully.

Steven ruffled his hair. "Thataway, son. I'm a meat-and-potatoes man myself, so that sure sounds good to me."

"Me, too." Tony was quick to include himself in this select male corps.

Samantha pictured the freezer's near-empty contents. She knew exactly what would happen if she admitted they were down to a few pounds of hamburger and some stew meat. Steamroller Steven would bulldoze his way past all her protests and talk her into accepting a month's worth of groceries. Then she would be even more beholden to him than she was now. "Maybe not my world-famous chicken, since it's not thawed, but I'm sure I can manage to come up with something filling."

"Thank you, ma'am," Steven tossed over his shoulder as he stationed his eager troops near the door. "Ready, men?"

"Ready."

Lifting Heather into her arms, Samantha watched the threesome march outside to do battle with the elements. "A man's got to do what a man's got to do," she informed her young daughter as she checked to make sure the door was closed firmly behind them.

Three hours later the troops returned, but the enlisted men fell asleep over their beef stew and weren't able to return to the front. Their commanding officer was kind enough to understand and helped Samantha carry the weary soldiers to bed. "They shoveled their little hearts out," he whispered to her over their sleeping heads, sounding more like a proud father than a relative stranger.

Samantha felt a painful twist in her chest as she watched him tuck in the covers and bestow a tender pat on each sleeping head. Not once since the twins were born had their own father displayed such open affection for them. Brad had been much too self-centered to bolster their burgeoning male egos and too concerned for his own entertainment to go out of his way to make fun for his sons. Yet, after only a few hours in their company, Steven Armstrong had managed to do all three of those things, and he was a man she'd always considered as self-centered as they come.

"Did I do something wrong?" Steven asked when he straightened up from the bed to find her staring holes through him.

To her horror Samantha felt the sting of tears in her eyes. "Don't be silly," she blurted hastily, then pushed the curtain aside and hurried back to the kitchen.

By the time Steven joined her, she had herself back under control, though her voice sounded brittle. "There's plenty more hot coffee in the pot if you want some. I'm going to put Heather down for her nap."

Steven scowled at the bedroom curtain as she and her sleepy daughter disappeared behind it. He didn't know what he'd done, but Samantha was acting all standoffish again. When she'd walked past him, she'd given him such a wide berth anyone would have thought he had some highly communicable disease.

He thought they'd gotten along great at lunch. They'd conversed on nonconsequential subjects, but he'd enjoyed it, and he thought she had, too. He was honest enough to admit that her sudden rejection of him hurt. He genuinely liked her, and he'd been hoping that she was coming to like him, as well.

He was still wondering about what he might have said or done to provoke her, as he poured himself another cup of coffee and then opened the refrigerator to find some milk. The old appliance had a short in it, for the light blinked on, then blinked right back off again. But in the brief moments of illumination, he was given an unbelievable picture.

He immediately set his coffee mug down on the nearest counter, then reached inside the refrigerator to tap the faulty bulb. As the light switched on, the unacceptable truth was confirmed. Except for a half-empty quart jar of milk, two eggs, a quarter pound of margarine, some cheese and an opened package of baloney, the refrigerator was empty!

Since Zack had volunteered to fetch all the ingredients he'd needed to cook breakfast that morning, Steven hadn't been aware of the meager food supplies available until now. He felt even worse when he opened the small freezer and found that it contained exactly three frozen packages of hamburger and a tray of ice cubes. He'd been appalled by the family's poor living conditions, but he'd never thought about the possibility that the only thing that stood between them and starvation was a few pounds of ground beef!

Recalling how many helpings of stew he'd consumed at lunch, Steven slammed the refrigerator door so hard that the cookie jar on top skittered over the side. Luckily he managed to catch it before it crashed to the floor, but his good fortune did nothing to alleviate his feelings of guilt. Or his extreme frustration with a certain perverse woman, Steven realized as he thought about those three innocent children asleep in the next room.

As soon as Samantha came through the curtain, her wrist was enclosed in an iron grip and her ear was subjected to a harsh whisper. "What the hell were you going to do once I ate you out of house and home? That damned, stubborn pride of yours won't feed those kids!''

Dragging her unwilling body across the kitchen floor, he yanked open the refrigerator door. ''Take a good look, lady!'' he rasped fiercely, doing his level best to convey his mounting anger toward her without waking the children. ''You're a good cook, but what the devil can you make out of that? What's on the menu for tonight, baloney soup?''

''Macaroni-and-cheese casserole, stewed carrots and bread pudding for dessert,'' Samantha whispered back just as fiercely.

Flabbergasted, Steven gaped down at her. ''What!''

''And if you don't like it, you're damned well welcome to leave!'' Lifting her chin defiantly, Samantha jerked her wrist out of his grasp and used her freed hand to slam the refrigerator door closed. It was either that, or she would've used it to slug her accoster, and the temptation to do that had been almost irresistible.

''I hate macaroni and cheese, but that's not the issue here, and you know it!'' Steven breathed through clenched teeth as he reached out automatically and caught the cookie jar on its second unscheduled drop to the floor.

''Well, my kids love it, and that *is* the issue.''

Carefully Steven returned the jar to its precarious position on top of the refrigerator, fighting off the urge he had to keep on slamming doors. Unfortunately the one on the refrigerator was the only door close enough to be of any help, and he wouldn't be able to live with himself if that damned cookie jar broke. Samantha might not feel bad over the loss of a few oatmeal cookies, but he wasn't about to snatch any more food out of those babies' mouths. "If you don't—"

"Shh!"

Casting a guilty look toward the bedroom, Steven drew in a deep breath and forced himself to keep his voice down. "If you don't want me to really lose my temper, you'll stop being deliberately obtuse," he hissed. "You're in a bad way here, and we both know it, and I'm going to do something about it whether you like it or not!"

Samantha planted her feet right in front of his, tipped up her chin belligerently and whispered back, "Is that so?"

"Yes, it is, and if you love those children, you'll stop behaving like an idiot and accept my help!"

"I don't need your help, and we don't accept charity."

"Well, you're going to accept it, even if I have to cram it down your stubborn throat," Steven murmured hoarsely, growing more and more furious with her childish obstinateness. "If I have anything to say about it, those kids won't spend another night in this freezing claptrap or go to bed hungry ever again. And if you're too proud to admit you need help, you don't deserve to be their mother."

This was the Steven Armstrong Samantha remembered, the arrogant jerk who thought he had the right to make decisions about other people's lives, a man who judged others without knowing the facts. Unfortunately Samantha didn't have the strength to combat him any longer, especially when he'd honed in on her greatest weakness—her children. As hard as she'd worked to make it otherwise, the house *was* cold, and only last night her loved ones *had* gone to bed hungry. If the less-than-adequate furnace died out completely, how long would it be before one of them got sick?

For all its lack of volume, Steven had never been involved in a bigger battle of wills. He couldn't recall a time when the force of his stare hadn't affected his opponent or when the bite of his temper hadn't left behind any visible marks. Never in his life had he been up against a female who was every bit as strong as himself, a tiny wisp of a woman who absolutely wouldn't back down.

He'd just about made up his mind to give up on this futile tactic and resort to some abject begging when he noted the small drop of moisture trickling down her cheek. At that moment the battle was won—and he was the loser. He reached for her before he could stop himself, wrapped his arms around her quivering shoulders and tucked her head beneath his chin. "Aw, hell, Samantha. Don't cry. Please don't cry. I have this terrible temper, but I never meant to hurt you. I wouldn't hurt you for anything in the world."

# Four

———

Everything will be all right, Samantha,'' Steven crooned, stroking her back as her tears soaked his shirtfront. With his arms around her, he was able to tell how delicate she was, how fragile, and he felt like a brute for upsetting her. "We'll figure something out."

Samantha drew in a deep quivering breath, hating herself for breaking down like this in front of him, but completely unable to stop crying. It was as if a dam inside her had burst, allowing all of her worries and fears to escape in one all-consuming rush of emotion. "Go away," she sobbed, but her arms were wrapped so tightly around his waist that he couldn't obey her even if he'd wanted to.

"I'm not going anywhere," Steven assured her.

Samantha stiffened her spine. The miserable cur wasn't going to allow her to salvage even a single scrap of her pride. "I . . . I never cry," she persisted brokenly. "Never."

Knowing how much she had to cry about, Steven swallowed the lump in his throat. "Then these must be all those tears you've got stored up," he replied in as matter-of-fact a tone as possible, and he drew her more closely against him.

"Go ahead and let them all out," he suggested softly. "Everyone has to cry sometime, and now is as good a time as any. I'm a pretty big guy, so don't worry that I'll wash away in the deluge."

His gentle words and protective action made Samantha cry all the harder. No matter how she felt about him, Steven Armstrong intended to be her anchor in the storm, and he wasn't going to give way until she'd weathered it. Held secure in his iron embrace, Samantha followed his suggestion and let go.

Steven had never felt such tenderness toward a woman before. He ached with it, but that wasn't the only ache he suffered. He hardly dared to breathe, for when he did, he inhaled the scent of delicate wildflowers that emanated from her silky blond hair. Whenever his chest expanded, he was excruciatingly aware of the soft, full womanly breasts pressed so intimately against him and the provocative tautness of their tips.

He knew that he couldn't take credit for the physical change that came over her breasts as they made contact with his body. Her nipples were hard little points, but it wasn't his touch that had caused their response. Such contraction was purely instinctive. Or was it?

Just when he thought he couldn't stand this torture another second, Steven realized that Samantha had stopped crying. He felt the alteration in her breathing, saw the pulse at the base of her neck beating wildly and heard the pleasurable gasp she made when he shifted his hips to relieve his increasing discomfort. Was she as sexually aware of him as he was of her?

He drew away, intending to question her, but the words were unnecessary. Her eyes were open, and there was a mesmerizing sensuality in their blue depths. He moved his gaze to her beautiful mouth and saw her lips part in anticipation. "I want to kiss you very badly," he groaned hoarsely, "but only if you want me to."

Samantha swallowed hard, her mouth growing dry as she tried to articulate her needs. She felt so exhausted and empty, so yearning, except where his hands were touching her. A pleasurable tingling was spreading outward from those areas, and she wanted to surrender her entire self to that warmth, to feel that heated sensation all over her body. She wanted to absorb his strength through her skin, energize herself with the vitality that radiated from him like the brilliant rays of a noonday sun.

"I . . . I do," she murmured, unable to convey anything but her acquiescence to his desire to kiss her.

Instantly his warm lips feathered across her jaw, then her cheek and finally her mouth. At first the kiss was merely warm, but in seconds Steven's mouth hardened, and the kiss became hot and hungry. Samantha felt his hands slide up around her neck, his fingers twining through her hair as he pulled her head back to gain deeper access to her mouth.

In that moment, everything changed. Comfort changed to pleasure, and solace inspired a growing need. Samantha had been kissed deeply before, but she'd never tasted such passion on a man's lips or felt such a thrilling heat in her own blood. His devouring mouth made demands, and she found herself obeying. As emotionally spent as she felt, she was more than willing to obey his demands, and in reward, she was pleasured by his bold, searching tongue.

"You taste so sweet," he murmured. "And you feel so good against me." Gliding his palms down her rib cage to her waist, then cupping her hips firmly, he pulled her into the muscular cradle of his thighs.

The heat of his touch rushed through her like wildfire, and suddenly the flickering passion inside her ignited into full flame. Samantha arched her spine, desperate to bring herself even closer. She wanted to feel the hard length of him pressing into her, and she lifted her body mindlessly, rubbing her breasts against him and shifting her hips to accommodate his arousal.

Steven groaned her name, and he began to move his hips with the same heedless compulsion that was driving her. He stole her breath when his mouth covered hers again, and his tongue slipped between her lips, searching, caressing, savoring her honeyed taste.

Steven felt the yielding in her body, and his brain stopped functioning on any rational level. All he knew was that he needed to touch her. Hesitantly he moved his hands up her rib cage to the soft, full curve of her breasts, then down again. When he felt no resistance in her, he insinuated his fingers into the soft folds of her shirt.

Samantha's body arched as he stroked her skin, and she made a tiny wild sound. When his fingers brushed against one nipple, she made it again. "I want you so badly it hurts," Steven growled softly just before taking her mouth again, but he was just as intent on satisfying her needs as he cupped both breasts in his hands.

Samantha moaned in pleasure, but Steven's response to her delight was an explosive yelp that tore their lips apart. His arms dropped away from her so abruptly that she stumbled and almost fell. Steven grabbed hold of her waist to steady her, and it was then that she realized what had happened to him, for it was about to happen again.

"Let go of my mommy, you bad man!" Heather exclaimed, prepared to kick him a second time if Steven didn't immediately comply with her fierce order.

Horrified, Samantha broke out of Steven's grasp and scooped the four-year-old Amazon up into her arms before she could inflict any more damage. "Heather Louise!"

Steven bent down to rub his injured shin, wincing as he fingered the bruise. "The little devil kicked me," he muttered in apparent disbelief.

Heather's small mouth pursed into an unrepentant pout as she eyed her dumbfounded victim. "You hurted my mommy," she accused angrily, one leg still swinging just in case Steven made a wrong move toward them. "And you maked her cry!"

Samantha swung around and carried her daughter quickly out of range. "Mr. Armstrong wasn't hurting me, Heather," she explained as she sat her daughter down on top of the kitchen table. "And he didn't make me cry. I was feeling sad, so he was giving me a nice big hug."

Heather frowned up into her mother's eyes, not completely trusting this explanation. "Then why'd you make all them funny noises, Mommy?"

Careful to keep his distance, Steven limped to the other side of the table and sat down in a chair. Heather's back was to him, but he was facing Samantha. Since he'd already received more than ample punishment for his part in this affair, he thought it only right that he was present when she got hers.

"You sounded like the kittens do when Zack rubs their fur the wrong way," Heather said, unaware of the amused grin on the face of the man seated behind her. "Was Mr. Armstrong rubbing you too hard?"

Steven cocked his head to one side and waited for Samantha to answer that one. She couldn't seem to think of a single thing to say, but her rosy blush was enough of an answer for Steven, whose grin grew even wider.

"Then was he squeezing you too tight?" Heather persisted when her mother remained silent.

Samantha grasped hold of that excuse like a lifeline, praying her small daughter wouldn't ask why her face was all red. "Maybe, just a little."

Heather nodded in sympathy. "When Zack hugs me too hard, I holler, too, even when I like it."

"I was not hollering, and I—" Samantha cut herself off before she got into even deeper trouble. The next time she opened her mouth, it was to scold, "What I was doing isn't the problem here, young lady!"

Confused by her mother's indignation, but certain that it had something to do with her kicking people, Heather gazed contritely over her shoulder. "I'm sorry, Steben."

"I'm sorry, Mr. Armstrong," Samantha corrected.

"I'm sorry, Mr.... Armstrong," Heather repeated obediently, then to make sure she was back in her mother's good graces, she promised magnanimously, "You can hug my mommy all you want, and I won't kick you even when she hollers."

*Oh Lord,* Samantha groaned silently and covered her burning face with her hands.

"Thank you, Heather," Steven managed to say without bursting out laughing. "And since I think you and I are going to be great friends, I'd like it if you called me Steven."

Heather smiled back at him shyly, slid off the table and went running for the bedroom. "Steben's my friend, too," she announced grandly as she disappeared behind the curtain.

Samantha lowered her hands, but not in time to ward off the muscular arms that lifted her off her feet and twirled her around. "You heard her, Samantha," Steven drawled wickedly, practically breaking her ribs as he hugged her. "I can hug you as hard as I want and not get kicked—Ow!"

Samantha landed back on her feet with a thud, but it wasn't hard enough to knock the smug smile off her face. "I taught my daughter everything she knows," Samantha informed him. "And *I* didn't promise you that."

"I stand corrected," Steven moaned pathetically, clutching his bruised shin. "On the only good leg I've got left."

Samantha giggled, but her amusement died a quick death when Steven looked at her and she saw the vengeful gleam in his dark eyes. "You only got what you deserve," she pointed out hastily.

While Samantha scanned the room, looking for a likely place to hide, Steven straightened back to his full height. With an evil chuckle, he warned, "And that's exactly what you're going to get."

He took a threatening step toward her, and Samantha took two quick steps back.

"You'd better run," he agreed as she scooted behind the kitchen table.

Samantha was fast on her feet and managed to continually frustrate his efforts to catch her by keeping the table between them. She was laughing so hard that he almost caught her on the second round, but her luck held. "You're not very coordinated," she teased breathlessly as he picked up the chair he'd just tripped over.

Steven wiggled his brows at her, then lunged over the table, catching her unawares. "Gotcha!" he exclaimed triumphantly as his fingers closed around her wrist. In seconds she was pulled into his arms, but was saved from whatever retaliation he intended by the sound of a helicopter hovering over the house.

"What rotten timing," Steven complained in frustration as they both heard the excited stirring from the next room.

Heather was the first to join them. "Hear that? It's the hellycopper! It's the hellycopper!"

Samantha smiled serenely as she stepped out of Steven's arms. "We heard."

"They saw our X," Zack shouted as he and Tony dashed out of the bedroom.

"C'mon, Steven," Tony called as he and his brother pulled on their coats. "Hurry up."

"I'm coming," Steven said, then whispered in Samantha's ear. "But I'll be back."

"Don't hurry on my account," Samantha replied sweetly as he walked away from her to fetch his jacket.

They were gone long enough for Samantha to relive the preceding hour over and over again in her mind. She'd experienced a wider range of emotions in the past sixty minutes than she had in the past year, and to her amazement, instead of feeling drained, she felt exhilarated.

She was actually looking forward to the moment when Steven walked back through the front door and picked up the gauntlet he'd tossed down when he'd left. "I must be cracking up," she stated out loud, unable to understand how she could possibly like a man whom she disliked so intensely. Or want him so badly when she didn't want him at all.

* * *

"I'm offering you a job, a perfectly respectable job!" Steven exclaimed in frustration, pacing up and down in front of the couch where Samantha was seated.

"Yes, I know, as your live-in...housekeeper." Samantha spat out the title as if it left a rotten taste in her mouth. "I know exactly what that job would entail, and I don't want it."

"Damn...darn it, Samantha!" Remembering their childish audience, Steven clenched his fists to stop himself from swearing. Since he'd spent the past several years living in an all-male household, it took one hell of an effort. "Working for me is a solution to your problems, and all you'd have to do is a little cooking and cleaning. If you'd kindly get your head up out of the gutter, you might be able to see some of the advantages in my offer."

Samantha's face flamed at the accusation, but she couldn't refute it without arousing even more anxiety in her already-anxious children. They'd been witness to more than enough adult arguments in their young lives without subjecting them to this. Fighting down the urge to sound sarcastic, she replied, "I truly appreciate your offer, Mr. Armstrong, but I can't accept it. As disadvantaged as we are, the children and I are doing just fine."

Steven glared across the table at her for several moments, glanced over at the three small worried faces, then stood up from the table. It was obvious that Samantha had dug in her heels about this, but she was about to learn that he could out-stubborn anybody.

"How'd you guys like to see the inside of a helicopter?" he asked the children, not in the least surprised by their answer.

Five minutes later, he and Samantha were able to continue where they'd left off without the presence of any eyewitnesses.

"Chuck's in his glory when he's showing off that whirlybird," he said as he hung his jacket back up on one of the pegs by the door. "And he loves kids."

Chuck Miller was nearing sixty and a confirmed bachelor. He'd announced that fact soon after Heather dumped four kittens into his lap, along with the information that he didn't have much experience dealing with babies. The poor man didn't know what to say or do when, with tears in her big blue eyes, Heather told him that the babies had just lost their mother, and that she couldn't be expected to look after all four of them when they grew up into cats. Not knowing how to refuse such a tearful entreaty, Chuck had staged a phony sneezing attack and made a quick exit.

"Sure he does," Samantha muttered dryly.

"They'll be fine with him," Steven assured her, lips twitching as he recalled the look of horror on his new foreman's craggy face as he'd deposited the three children inside the helicopter and told Chuck that he would be baby-sitting until further notice.

Samantha was standing at the stove and had her back to him. She didn't turn around as she warned him, "I've made up my mind about this, Steven, and whatever you've got to say that couldn't be said in front of the children won't change it."

"We'll see about that."

"Yes, we will."

Steven had the legal right to kick her off his land, and if she kept this up, he just might do it yet. "If you aren't willing to listen, I can always resort to action instead of words."

Mistaking his meaning, Samantha whirled around to face him. "Are you threatening me?"

Steven watched her chin come up like a prize fighter daring his opponent to throw his best punch. He recognized the aggressive stance, for she'd looked the same way the night before when she'd come upon him in the barn. Like then, she didn't seem to be aware that he was twice her size, and he found that oversight highly endearing. "Would it do any good if I was?"

"No!"

"I didn't think so." Steven plunked himself down at the kitchen table and fortified himself with a cup of coffee. This was going to be an uphill battle every step of the way. "So if threats won't work, what will? How about bribery? I'll double my previous offer."

Samantha's face went pale as he named an outrageous sum, unknowingly confirming her worst suspicions. With that kind of money to throw around, he didn't need to hire an amateur housekeeper who came with three kids, ten cows and four kittens. "Why can't you just accept the fact that I don't want the job?"

"Why can't *you* accept the fact that you don't have much choice? Your kids need food in their stomachs and a decent roof over their heads, and if what those heifers have is contagious, you're in danger of losing all your stock. Then where will you be?"

Samantha sat down in the chair opposite his. "That's my worry, not yours."

"Accept my offer, and your worries are over."

*Or just beginning,* Samantha thought. After this afternoon's impassioned episode, she knew if she went to live in his house, sooner or later she would end up in his bed. The man had a reputation for preferring blondes, and now her name headed the list. Steven wanted her. Even if he hadn't said it while they were kissing, she could read that knowledge in his eyes whenever he looked at her. Oh, yes, he was willing to pay for her services as a housekeeper, but he would place a much greater value on her service to him as a lover.

He didn't have any idea how good a housekeeper she was, and he obviously didn't care. Knowing that, if she accepted the job, what would it make her? "I said no, and I mean no! The children and I belong here, and this is where we're staying. It's a struggle right now, but we'll get by."

"If I didn't know better, I'd think you were related to the stubborn old coot who used to live here," Steven bit out acidly, angered by her totally irrational refusal of his more-than-generous offer. "Caleb Todd stored his brains inside a whiskey bottle, so I understood why he couldn't think straight. What's your excuse?"

"You don't know half as much as you think," Samantha retorted furiously. "Caleb Todd was my father, and his refusal to sell out to you was the most intelligent decision any man ever made, drunk or sober."

"You...you're that cantankerous old fool's daughter!"

Caleb Todd *was* a cantankerous old fool, but Samantha didn't want to hear it from the likes of Steven Armstrong. All the hostility she'd harbored against him as a child came to the fore. "Yes, I am, and if you think you had trouble trying to buy this land away from him, you just try getting it from me. I'd rather starve than sell out to you!"

Steven heard but chose to ignore that heated challenge, still stunned by the news of her identity. "You're that crazy little urchin who used to pitch rocks at my head and spook my horse whenever you saw me?"

"I only saw you a few times," Samantha came back defensively, remembering why their fourth encounter had been their last. She'd been perched on top of a low cliff when he'd ridden past, and she'd tossed a small stone over the edge. His horse had reared and bucked him off into a nearby thornbush. Luckily he'd come up fighting mad, but Samantha had realized how badly he might have been hurt. From that day forward, she'd gone out of her way to avoid running into him again.

Steven was caught up in his own memories, thinking back to the plucky little girl who'd defended her no-account father with every weapon at her disposal. He could never figure out why she felt such fierce loyalty toward a man who'd never worked an honest day in his life, but she certainly had. He'd only spoken to the girl once, but somehow he'd managed to make her into a bitter enemy.

As he recalled, he'd been in a foul mood that day due to his most recent dealings with Caleb. The man had frustrated him so badly he'd had a crashing headache. He still couldn't remember exactly what he'd said to set her off, but he had to assume he'd insulted her persnickety old man. Afterward he'd been in danger from her arsenal of sticks and stones every time he'd ridden onto their property. If he'd managed to catch her, he would have tanned her bottom good, but she'd always hightailed it out of sight before he'd recovered from the surprise attack.

As for her shiftless father, he'd continually defied every effort Steven's family had made to help him out of his financial troubles. His section of land was too small to support a working ranch, but Caleb didn't seem to mind. His more prosperous neighbors could have used some prime additional pasture, and the profit Caleb would have made on the deal would have set him up nicely in town, but for some perverse reason, Caleb didn't want them to have it. Year after year, the Armstrongs offered to buy, and year after year, he'd taken an almost maniacal delight in rejecting their offers.

After each rejection he'd dangled the possibility that he might consider selling out at a better price, but as soon as they'd agreed to the higher figure, he would up the price again. Ironically the pleasure he'd gained from thwarting the Armstrongs had eventually been overtaken by his need for another kind of gratification, and in the end he'd sold out to them for a couple of thousand dollars and a case of fine whiskey.

Now that he knew who Samantha was, Steven understood her initial hostility toward him. Caleb Todd had never been closemouthed about his feelings for the Armstrongs, and his daughter had been taught to share them. If Samantha found out that he was the owner of her land, he would really be in for it.

The last thing he wanted to inspire in her was more anger, so he decided to keep that lethal piece of information to himself for a while longer. "My, my, how you've changed," he drawled, hoping to divert the conversation away from the issue of land ownership. "And all for the better, I might add."

"Well, you haven't changed at all," Samantha said, blue eyes sparkling defiantly. "You still feel free to trounce all over other people's feelings in order to get what you want. Today you've decided I'm to be your housekeeper, and you'll say or do anything to force me into accepting, no matter how I might feel about the matter."

With a flushed face, she exclaimed melodramatically, "Lord only knows what you'll want from me next!"

Steven cocked an astonished brow at her. "Is that what's behind all this? You honestly think I intend to make you my mistress even if you don't like the idea?"

"I most certainly do!"

Steven considered the possibility that she could be right, then swiftly discarded it. He might want her in his bed, but he would never force her into doing something that went against what she wanted, and he was hurt by her misjudgment of him. "When I make love to a woman, she has to want it as much as I do,'' he informed her quietly.

"So you can see why I can't possibly work for you."

Now he was really confused. "Huh?"

"You can make me want you even when I know it's wrong. Just look what happened this afternoon?" She spat in self-disgust. "You kissed me, and before I knew it, we were all over each other. How long do you think I could hold out, if you *really* made an effort to seduce me?"

Steven's mouth gaped open as she rushed on, providing him with her own answer. "Not long enough, that's for sure."

Having worked up a good head of steam, Samantha kept on rolling, and Steven made no attempt to stand in her way. The woman was priceless, absolutely priceless, and he would have paid a king's ransom for the insights into her personality that she was handing over to him free of charge. "You're a very sexy man, and I'd probably enjoy sleeping with you very much, but I've got three impressionable children to raise," she informed him tartly. "If I don't set a good example for them, they'll make all the same mistakes I have, and I absolutely refuse to let that happen!"

Samantha paused for breath, but then took up the one-sided conversation again. "I didn't learn my lesson until I was an adult, but my daughter's going to be taught that she doesn't need a man to lean on in order to survive. Unlike my father and husband, my sons are going to find out that hard work is good for both the body and the soul. My children are going to understand that the only person they can always count on is themselves. Therefore, I won't become your mistress, and after today, we won't be accepting any more favors from you."

"I see," Steven remarked at the conclusion of her tirade, trying to sound noncommittal as his whirling brain struggled to assimilate all the information it had just received.

"Good," Samantha replied, feeling deflated as she slumped back in her chair. "I'm glad that's settled."

"It is," Steven confirmed, turning thoughtful as he leaned back in his own chair. Nothing was settled as far as he was concerned, but he wasn't about to risk another angry outburst by telling her so. There had to be some way of getting around all of her objections, some way of convincing her that she wouldn't be compromising her principles if she came to work for him, but what was it?

Silence reigned between them for several moments, but then it was broken by a loud bang followed by a prolonged wheezing sound. "What the hell was that!" Steven demanded as he shot to his feet.

"Oh, no." Samantha's shoulders slumped in defeat, and she lifted one hand to her forehead, hoping to rub away the sudden sharp pain centered there.

"Samantha!"

"The lousy furnace just died," she moaned without looking at him. If she had, she would've seen Steven's anxious expression replaced by a brilliant smile.

# Five

———

Steven adjusted his legs to provide a more comfortable position for the tiny girl he held on his lap, and he glanced over his shoulder at the three passengers in the rear seat of the helicopter. He had to shout in order to be heard over the noise of the whirling blades. "How are you guys doing back there?"

"We're doing fine," Samantha shouted in answer to what she felt was an unnecessary question. Any blind man could see that they were better than fine. At least the twins were, she added mentally. If not for the seat belts they were wearing, the boys would be jumping up and down for joy.

Steven wasn't fooled by Samantha's positive response. Nope, the lady was none too happy with the recent turn of events. He, on the other hand, couldn't be happier. Very soon, he was going to have Samantha Charles on his territory, and if he had anything to say about it, she wouldn't be going back to that run-down cabin any time soon. She and her children were going to sleep well and eat right for a change.

"Ever flown in one of these before?" he inquired pleasantly, hoping to ease the tension between them, but the question earned him such a fierce glare that he decided further conversation could wait until after they landed.

"Gosh! Everything looks so little from up here," Tony exclaimed excitedly. "'Cept'n the mountains. See how close we are! Seems like we could reach out the window and touch them rocks."

Samantha's stomach lurched at the thought, but she refused to show her fear as the helicopter swerved between two towering cliffs and zoomed up over a granite ledge. The late-afternoon sun cast long shadows over the snow, and the jagged rocks and jutting peaks looked cold, dark and sinister. A shiver of anxiety snaked down her spine, but she managed to sound enthusiastic. "If there wasn't so much snow, we could probably count the needles on those pine trees."

"Look at that, Mom," Zack cried. "We're up so high, we're flying through a cloud."

"Nah, that's just fog," Tony disputed his brother's claim. "Isn't it, Mom?"

Even though she was terrified, Samantha forced herself to look out the window again. As the copter dipped down over the next tree-covered ridge, it passed through a pocket of white mist. "Fog is a kind of cloud, Tony. It's made up of water vapor, but fog hovers closer to the ground, and clouds are formed up in the sky." *Please let it be fog,* she prayed silently, then noting just how low they were flying, she quickly added, *Only don't let us be that close to the ground.*

"Told ya," Zack retorted smugly. "We're flying through a cloud."

Tony was about to say that they couldn't count fog as a real cloud, but Steven distracted him with an order to look down. "We're coming up on the old homestead," he announced jovially. "That building that looks like it's made out of Lincoln Logs is the house, and the one with the brown roof is the big barn."

"Wow!" both boys shouted together, their noses glued to the window.

Samantha felt the same way over what she saw, but she kept her exclamation to herself. Even though everything appeared to be constructed in miniature, the Triple A Ranch consisted of much more than a house and a barn. Along with several more snow-topped barns, she could see neatly fenced paddocks, three low-slung aluminum sheds and four silos. Next to the house was a garage that had to be wide enough to hold several cars, and in the clearing on the other side was the outline of a kidney-shaped swimming pool, a cabana-like building and a fenced-off area that she assumed housed a tennis court.

The old homestead had changed a lot since the days when Steven's father had been in charge. Samantha had only seen the place from afar, but she couldn't recall half the buildings nor the recreational facilities being there when she'd last viewed it. Evidently, since succeeding Hunter Armstrong at the helm of Armstrong Enterprises, Steven had far exceeded him in profit making.

Or maybe father and son had a different set of priorities, she thought, remembering that Hunter had been a member of the old school of ranchers who'd highly disapproved of any newfangled developments. She bet the man would roll over in his grave if he knew that today his son rode the range in a helicopter and played a sissy game like tennis after a hard day's work.

Samantha smiled to herself as she fancied that confrontation, but she wasn't given much chance to enjoy the picture, for Chuck announced that they were about to land. Samantha felt her stomach fall as the helicopter descended to the ground with one downward whoosh, and she didn't open her eyes again until she heard the propeller stop rotating. "We made it," she murmured in surprise.

"Was there some doubt in your mind?" Steven teased, but he didn't wait for her answer as he pushed open the door and jumped out.

Samantha's heart did a somersault as he smiled back up at her. The man looked so blasted happy, it was almost impossible not to return his smile. "It wouldn't crack your face, you know," he teased, demonstrating his uncanny ability to read her mind.

Fearing what else he might see in her expression, Samantha turned away to unfasten the boys' seat belts. As they scrambled over her legs, she stole a second glance out the open door, and her heart did another flip-flop. Steven was still standing there, and he was still smiling at her.

Samantha tried, but she couldn't get over the impression that he looked like a glad father, welcoming his wife and children back home after a long trip. He was holding Heather effortlessly in the crook of one strong arm, and the little girl was fast asleep, her blond head nestled contentedly against his broad shoulder, her chubby arms wrapped around his neck. The child looked serenely content and didn't stir even when Steven reached out his hand and swung, first Tony, then Zack, down to the snow-packed ground.

Neither boy hesitated for a second as they grabbed hold of his hand, demonstrating the kind of trust Steven had fostered in them after so short a time. It was instinctive, as if they knew they couldn't get hurt while in his care, that in times of trouble, he could be counted on to take charge—which was exactly what he'd done since the moment he'd entered their lives.

To her sons, he must seem so big and strong and tough, a stable presence in an uncertain world. Samantha could see the adoration in their eyes as they gazed up at him, and she worried that they were already too attached to him. She didn't want them to think that Steven was going to play any major role in their lives, because he wasn't. They would only be staying with him for a day or two, just until the furnace was fixed. Then they would go back to where they belonged, and Steven Armstrong could just—

"Do you need some help getting down?" Steven asked, holding out his hand to her.

"No, thanks," Samantha replied with the same answer she always gave his offers. His amused chuckle told her that he was coming to expect that response from her whenever he extended a helping hand, but he wasn't going to let it bother him. At least, not this time.

"Suit yourself," he said, his twinkling brown eyes beaming the message that he was more than satisfied with the concessions she'd already made to him today. *I'll let you win the small ones,* his laughing eyes seemed to say. *As long as I keep winning the big ones.*

Over the next few minutes, Samantha felt like a soldier who'd just been drafted against her will into this man's army. Steven barked out orders, and those under his command hurried to comply, that is, all but one. Unlike the boys, Samantha took her time marching over to the waiting Jeep, and when she was told to get inside where it was warm, she refused, even when Steven handed Heather over to her.

"Sit tight, honey," she told her daughter, who came awake as Samantha sat her down next to Zack in the back seat.

Closing the door on Heather's protests, she straightened up and stared over the Jeep's hood at Steven. She'd seen the warning glance he'd directed at his foreman when he'd brought up the subject of her ailing cattle, and she wanted to hear the rest of their conversation. If he was planning to overstep his bounds where her stock was concerned, he'd better think again. Whatever was wrong with those heifers, it was her problem, and she would decide how to deal with it.

"I should have thought to have you look at them when we were there," Steven said. "They were kicking their bellies." He tossed Samantha's large suitcase and two smaller ones onto the top carrier and lashed them down with a rope.

Chuck motioned Tony to roll down the rear window and handed him the basket of kittens. "Not colic?"

"Not colic," Steven agreed.

"Pinched their withers?"

"Nothing."

"Any show?"

"Yup," Steven said. "I'll want a track plowed over there by nightfall."

Chuck nodded as if that were a foregone conclusion.

The brief exchange had been conducted in English, but it could have been in Chinese for all Samantha understood. Asking for a translation would be like an admission of ignorance, so if she didn't want them to know that she didn't have a clue why cows kicked their bellies, she had no choice but to remain silent. She almost spoke up when Chuck said, "We can board them in the third barn," but Steven negated that suggestion before Samantha got the chance.

"Samantha thinks it would be too much trouble for us to haul them over here, even though we'll need the truck to retrieve Challenger," he said, a long-suffering expression on his face. "Until the vet can get out there, all she wants us to do is inject them with some antibiotics. Three times a day ought to do it."

Samantha colored slightly when Chuck threw her a frowning glance. Considering how things had turned out, her restrictions were causing Steven more trouble than he would have had without them. She certainly couldn't expect him, or one of his men, to attend to her sick cows three times a day. "If it would make the work easier, you can bring the heifers back here."

Steven bit back his triumphant smile. "It would make the work easier if we loaded up all your animals. Then we wouldn't have to trek out there day and night in order to feed and water them. You can't go back until the furnace is fixed, and who knows how long that will take."

The man had her over a barrel, and he knew it, Samantha thought resentfully. She still didn't want his charity, but if she turned this offer down, his foreman would think she was not only selfish, but ungrateful, as well. "Okay, but I insist on paying you back for boarding them, and for whatever feed they eat while they're here."

Chuck gazed at her as if she were crazy for looking a gift horse like Steven in the mouth, but all he said was, "We should be back here around midnight."

Steven nodded. "Give those heifers their first injection before you load them up. My guess is pyelonephritis."

*Pyelo... what?* Samantha had never heard of such a thing, and it sounded deadly serious. What if her heifers were victims of some kind of virulent cow plague? If pyelo-something-or-other was contagious, she could lose the entire herd.

Chuck said, "I'll tell Mike to break out the penicillin."

"That ought to do the trick," Steven agreed. "Don't you think so, Samantha?"

"That would be my choice," Samantha said, trying to sound more knowledgeable than relieved. She was fast learning that she didn't know half as much about her business as she should, but her pride couldn't stand it if Steven ever found that out. Then another thought occurred to her that lifted her spirits. Some good just might come out of this after all.

While her stock was being boarded here, she would have a good excuse to be in the barn. What she didn't know, she could learn. If she asked the right questions and listened to some of the stockmen, she could gain herself a free education.

"Okay, get on it, Chuck," Steven said as he opened the driver's-side door. "And take a look at that furnace while you're out there in case we need to order parts. I don't think it can be saved, but you'd know that better than I."

"Will do."

"Is there anything else you want him to do, Samantha?" Steven asked, but she was already seated inside the Jeep and didn't hear his question. "Didn't think so," he muttered under his breath, smiling as he slid beneath the wheel and put the Jeep in gear.

Not much was said as Steven maneuvered the Jeep over the recently plowed road that led from the landing site to the house. All of his concentration was needed not to slide off the icy track. The children's attention was directed out the windows as they took in their new surroundings, and Samantha spent the trip trying to keep her eyes off their driver.

She didn't have much success, for there was something about Steven that drew her gaze like a magnet.

His tan Stetson was pulled down at a rakish angle over his forehead, and in his sheepskin jacket, worn jeans and boots, he looked like a very sexy cowboy, even though he was driving a Jeep, not riding a horse. Still, as Samantha watched his gloved hands on the wheel, she decided that he probably rode like he drove. His movements were certain and controlled. He had expert hands that could master the erratic movements of a car, a horse...or a woman, with equal skill.

As she remembered the feel of those hands on her breasts, the gentle possession of his palms, Samantha began to feel uncomfortably warm. When she recalled the delicious feel of his warm fingers on her soft skin, her nipples hardened, and she crossed her arms defensively over her chest. Even the memory of his touch excited her so much that her body reacted instantly, and no matter how much she disliked admitting it, she wanted more.

She cast a longing gaze at his mouth and found herself fantasizing on how it would feel closing over her breast. She knew that his lips and tongue would be as sensually skillful as his fingers. With agonizing slowness he would draw one nipple into his mouth and play her with an expert touch, incite her passion until she was begging him to soothe the tormenting ache he'd created deep within her.

A jolt of sheer panic brought an abrupt halt to her erotic reverie. What was she going to do if her fantasy became reality? Her spirit was strong, but her flesh was traitorously weak, and she couldn't seem to fight the sensations that overcame her each time she looked at the man. It was fast coming clear to her that, around him she became a spineless wimp.

"Still pouting?" Steven inquired when he heard her exasperated sigh, frowning as he glanced over at her and saw her defensive posture. He knew enough about body language to figure out what her crossed arms and stiff backbone meant. She would rather be anywhere else but here with him. "Is the thought of staying with me for a couple of days really that bad?"

Samantha was so grateful that he'd misjudged the cause of her agitation that she couldn't suppress a grin. "Are you kidding? I feel like I've just won a contest, and the prize is a free, getaway weekend at a swanky mountain lodge. That's some place you've got there, Steven."

Steven tightened his hands on the steering wheel. The woman was deliberately trying to annoy him. She knew what he was asking. He wanted to know how she felt about staying with him, and she'd neatly sidestepped the question with this phony show of excitement over his house. "Thanks," he returned shortly.

"I can't wait to see the inside," she declared in the same overly bright tone. "How many rooms does it contain?"

Steven shrugged as if to say he'd never counted. "Twenty or so," he muttered vaguely, then attempted once more to introduce a more personal note.

"Enough to make it seem very empty when I'm home alone," he said, hoping to gain some indication that she was more interested in the man than in his house.

The attempt failed. "How many bedrooms?"

"Six, not including the master suite," Steven replied, giving up. "There's plenty of room."

"And I bet every one of them is beautifully decorated," Samantha said, thinking of her own cramped house that was furnished in early garage-sale.

To her surprise Steven cleared his throat and looked highly uncomfortable. "I wouldn't know about that. My mother furnished the house, and I haven't changed much of anything since she died."

"I'm sure she had exquisite taste."

"Yes, she did," Steven replied, but if anything, her reference to his mother made him squirm even more. "If she were here, everything in the house would look perfect...but...well...the rooms aren't exactly ready for guests. I wasn't expecting company, so things are sort of messy."

Samantha gazed out the window at his house, compared it to her own and laughed out loud, which earned her a fierce scowl. "Sorry," she giggled. "But if you remember where you slept last night, that's really funny. The only accommodations I had to offer you were a lumpy couch or a stall in the barn."

Pointing out the window at his huge home, she teased, "I don't know why, but somehow I think the kids and I are going to get better than we gave."

"That's a matter of opinion," Steven muttered so softly that Samantha almost didn't hear him. She glanced over at him and could have sworn he was blushing, but she didn't have a chance to question that possibility.

Steven pulled up before the front door of the house and was out of the car almost before the motor had stopped running. The kids were just as quick to vacate the back seat, and they were halfway up the walk before Samantha had her door open. "Come back here," she called after them. "We have to help Steven with the luggage. Zack, you can take in the kittens, and, Tony, you carry one of the small suitcases, and I'll take the other one. Heather, you can carry Mommy's purse."

"That's all right, Samantha. If you take the kittens, I can get everything else," Steven said as he untied the rope on the top carrier.

She whirled around to face him. They'd barely gotten here, and what she feared would happen had started already. "No, it's not all right," she snapped. "The children are going to help carry in the luggage."

Steven didn't think that she saw him roll his eyes as he handed down one of the small bags to Tony, but she had. She also heard the commiserating giggle he got in return from her son, and she didn't like it one bit. The man's mocking reaction to her philosophy of child rearing was exactly the kind of thing she was most worried about.

She realized that all he wanted to do was to make life a little easier for the children, but they had to learn that life wasn't always easy. Anyone who wanted to succeed in this world had to be self-disciplined and pull his or her own weight, and it was her responsibility as a parent to teach this lesson. If she gave way on small things, they would soon expect her to give way on larger ones, as well.

Samantha knew from experience what happened to people who were never taught to consider others before themselves. She'd been married to just such a man, and he'd walked out on her and his three children without a backward glance and with no means of support. Brad's sole concern had been his own happiness, and when he'd found a new woman, who made no demands on him, he'd cut all ties with the old one. If nothing else, Samantha was going to make sure that her children felt a sense of responsibility for their own actions, whether they were good ones or bad.

Unfortunately the boys automatically looked up to Steven, and she'd just discovered that he wasn't past undermining her authority in subtle ways. This time, she wouldn't comment on his tactics, but heaven help him if he ridiculed her standards again. "Is that everything?"

"Yes, ma'am!" Steven gave her a smart salute as he picked up her large suitcase.

"Now we won't have to make a second trip," she declared primly, but she doubted that any of the four individuals who dashed ahead of her up the walk had heard. With an indignant sniff of her nose, Samantha followed behind them.

As soon as Steven shouldered open the door, Samantha realized why he'd seemed so uncomfortable during their recent conversation about their respective homes. Hers might have only one room compared to his twenty, and it had been furnished poorly, but every nook and cranny was clean. Steven's home had a zillion more nooks and crannies, and as far as she could tell, every one of them was filthy!

Her eyes growing wider with each step, she allowed him to usher her into the large, shockingly messy living room. It was indeed beautifully decorated with solid, masculine furniture, but there had to be a quarter inch of dust on each piece. Dirty dishes and old newspapers were lying all over the place, and the braided rugs on the dark hardwood floor looked as if they hadn't been vacuumed in months.

"I told you I wasn't prepared for guests," Steven reminded her, a sheepish expression on his face. "And I wasn't lying when I told you that I needed a housekeeper."

Unlike Samantha, who was too stunned to move away from the doorway, the children made themselves right at home. "Wow! A big-screen television," Zack exclaimed, brushing several newspapers off the brown leather couch to make room for himself and his brother. "Can we watch it, Steven?"

"And a VCR," Tony added, staring with awe at the entertainment center built in next to the large stone fireplace. "Can we watch a movie?"

"Sure." Steven seemed more than anxious to comply with their request, and Samantha was too busy taking in the atrocious condition of the room to try to stop him. Moments later, all three children were seated in a row on the couch, happily viewing the hard-luck adventures of a scruffy little dog on the wide screen.

Samantha came out of her daze when the movie started, for it provided her with another reason to be amazed. She never would have expected Steven to be the type to enjoy such a sentimental picture. Her face must have shown it, for when he caught her staring at him, he explained, "I've always had a soft spot for dogs. I still can't make it through *Lassie Come Home* without using up a half a box of tissues."

Samantha couldn't picture him crying his eyes out over a fictional dog, nor a real one for that matter, but she was just as certain that he was telling the truth. As hard as she tried not to be affected, the admittance endeared him to her, and she smiled in sympathy. "It takes me a whole box."

Steven had bent over to pick up her suitcase, intending to carry it upstairs, but his head jerked up at her soft tone. As he searched her liquid blue eyes, he felt himself lose all grip on his senses, just the way he lost his grip on the suitcase, which landed with a loud thump on the floor.

"Is something wrong?" Samantha asked, her smile faltering.

Steven shook his head, wishing he could think of something to say that would make her smile at him again. The sight of it warmed the blood in his veins and caused his heartbeat to speed up. It made him think that she might not consider him such a bad guy after all. And, if she got to know him better, she might even decide she could like him a lot.

He'd never gone out of his way to make a woman like him before, but with this one, he was willing to do almost anything to convince her that he was her friend. At the same moment as he entertained that high-minded thought, he heard his conscience scoff. *You're not fooling me, buddy. You want to be much more than her friend!*

"Nothing's wrong," he assured her huskily, but he couldn't quite control his errant eyes. They traced the delicate lines of her face and lingered hungrily on her mouth.

Samantha moistened her suddenly dry lips. "Oh . . . well . . . you looked kind of funny."

Steven smiled a wicked, purely male smile. "That's because you make me feel kind of funny."

His dark eyes moved to her breasts, and Samantha gasped. "Steven Armstrong!" she whispered fiercely, darting a quick glance at the children to make sure they weren't watching them. "Don't you dare start!"

"Start what?" Steven inquired innocently.

"Behaving like a lech!"

"I'm stung!" Steven winced as if in pain, but then he grinned. "At least now I know what I'll find once I get past all those prickles of yours. A woman who cries over Lassie has to have a soft heart."

Samantha's lips parted on a rush of breath. "I'm not sure what I'll find under that macho exterior of yours."

Steven took a step toward her, challenged by the passionate fire in her eyes, but just in time he remembered that she had some very strong feelings about the children witnessing any physical displays of affection. If he wanted this visit to last for more than five minutes, he had to keep his hands off her.

With difficulty he tore his eyes away from her. "I'll bring this suitcase upstairs, then I'd better clean things up a bit in the kitchen. It's almost supper time, and you're probably getting hungry."

"You don't have to go to any fuss," Samantha told him, bending down to reach for the handle of her case.

"And I can carry this upstairs. Just tell me which room you want us to use."

"No!" Steven pulled the suitcase out of her grasp and started backing out of the room.

Samantha saw that he was wearing the same uncomfortable expression that he'd worn earlier in the car. "You and the kids can have the first two rooms at the top of the stairs," he announced. "But I don't want you to see...eh...I mean I'm not sure there's fresh bedding on all the beds. Why don't you let me make sure everything's shipshape before you come up."

"Okay," Samantha agreed, biting her lip to keep from laughing as she watched him sprint down the hall and take the stairs to the second floor two steps at a time. Who would have thought a corporate giant could be so fast on his feet or so endearingly anxious to please a peon like her?

# Six

---

You understand then, that this is strictly temporary? As soon as my furnace is fixed or a new one installed, the kids and I will be going home," Samantha said that evening as she accepted the snifter of brandy Steven held out to her. She expected him to sit down next to her on the couch, and she tried not to seem nervous at the prospect, but she needn't have worried. Steven turned his back on her and walked away toward the fireplace.

According to the rigid set of his shoulders and spine, he didn't like what he was hearing, but Samantha didn't care. If he wanted her help, he would have to accept her conditions. "I'll be your housekeeper, but only on a day-to-day basis in exchange for our room and board."

Steven's jaw went tight. "Since I invited all four of you to stay here for as long as you like, room and board isn't a consideration in this discussion. I expect to pay you a salary."

"That's very nice of you," Samantha said, willing to concede that point. Even if she *did* feel guilty about accepting Steven's hospitality for an indefinite period of time, she needed the money this job would afford her. A new furnace was going to cost a considerable amount, and her savings were nil. "You can pay me by the hour, and I'll make up a time sheet to show when I'm working and when I'm not. Agreed?"

Steven placed his glass down on the oak mantel. Before responding to her question, he reached for the iron poker and shifted the burning logs until they flamed more brightly. "Keeping track of your hours will only add to the amount of paperwork I have to deal with as it is. Let's keep this simple. I know what the job is worth. The last woman I hired agreed to sign on for a month if I paid her in advance. Wouldn't you rather do that?"

"Didn't you tell me that the last woman you hired took off after only three days?"

"She took off because I fired her, but she had a whole month's salary to tide her over until she got another job."

"I'd rather get paid for work I really do."

Steven sighed. He could argue all he wanted, but he knew it wouldn't do him any good. Considering her upbringing, he had no idea where Samantha had come by such lofty standards, but he couldn't help but admire her integrity. "You've seen the lousy condition of this house. If those are your terms, I'll have to agree."

Samantha was astonished that he'd given up so quickly, and it made her suspicious. A man in Steven's position was used to having his wishes followed, so why was he suddenly being so agreeable? She felt even less sure about her decision to accept this job when she realized that he'd been in this conciliatory mood ever since her furnace had died, leaving her and the children with no choice but to stay with him until it was fixed or the weather warmed up. "Those are my terms for employment," she said firmly, stressing the last word, just so there was no mistake about their future relationship.

"Very well," Steven said. He told her the hourly wage he intended to pay.

It was much too generous an amount, but Samantha could see that he wasn't going to budge on that point. "That's too high," she felt obliged to say. "But I'd be a fool to turn it down."

Steven picked up his glass of brandy and saluted her. "Then consider yourself hired, Mrs. Charles."

Samantha inclined her head in acknowledgment of the gesture. "I can get started first thing in the morning."

"That will be fine," Steven said, then bent down, using one hand to pick up a log and toss it on the fire.

Samantha watched the effortless motion of his long body, the ease with which he handled the heavy wood. Steven didn't seem the least bit tired, while exhaustion was rapidly overtaking her. She was having trouble keeping her eyes open, but she hadn't dared go up

to bed until they'd worked out all the details of their arrangement. As soon as she'd seen the deplorable condition of Steven's kitchen, she'd had second thoughts about turning down his job offer, but it was the tasteless meal he'd prepared that had clinched the matter in his favor. Even so, she wanted it clear from the beginning that they were speaking short-term, just as he'd insisted on paying her that exorbitant hourly wage.

Stifling a yawn, she said, "When would you like breakfast on the table?"

Normally Steven was up and out of the house by seven in the morning, but when he saw her yawn, he replied, "I don't have to be in Billings until noon. How about nine-thirty?"

"Nine-thirty it is," she replied crisply, trying to keep the pleasure at being able to sleep in out of her voice.

Steven walked over to the couch, making sure he didn't sit down too close to her. He would have liked nothing better than to take her into his arms, but things were going much too well for him to do anything to jeopardize it. "Now that we've concluded our business, let's settle back and enjoy our brandy. It's been a long day."

"Yes, it has," Samantha agreed, struggling to stay awake. Thinking it might help, she took a tentative sip. The fiery liquid burned her throat, but she was surprised by how good it tasted. Having lived with an alcoholic father, she'd always avoided liquor. She hadn't felt she'd had anything to prove to her friends, but tonight the circumstances were different.

Tonight she'd wanted to appear worldly wise and sophisticated when Steven had suggested that they retire to the living room to talk and enjoy a nightcap once the children were in bed. Steven had spoken the refined phrase, "retire to the living room," in such an elegant tone of voice that she'd immediately been reminded of the difference in their backgrounds. If they'd been two characters in the Regency romance novels she enjoyed, the "ton" would definitely have considered her far beneath his station.

As a teenager she'd thought that, too. She'd been about fourteen the first time she'd ventured near enough to view this magnificent house, and even though she'd never seen it from the inside, she'd assumed it was wonderful. Back then, she'd tried to imagine what it would be like living here, what life would be like among the wealthy Armstrongs. One of her expectations had been right on target. After dinner, rich, classy people reclined on luxurious leather couches before a romantic fire and drank expensive brandy out of fine lead-crystal snifters.

With a dreamy sigh, Samantha took a larger swallow of her drink and savored the pleasant feeling of warmth that spread through her body. As she leaned back against the plush cushions of the couch and gazed into the fire, she realized that she was beginning to feel entirely too relaxed and comfortable in this setting. Compared to the lord of the manor, she might be a lowly peasant, but she could learn to like this lifestyle. She could learn to like it far too much.

Steven saw Samantha's eyelids flutter, then close, and he reached out for her glass before she spilled the remaining contents into her lap. When he moved closer to take it from her grasp, the cushion dipped, and a sleeping Samantha slid across the smooth leather back of the couch. Steven lifted his arm, and her head came to rest on his chest.

A gentleman wouldn't have taken advantage of such a situation, but Steven couldn't resist the temptation to cuddle. It felt so good to hold her, and where she was concerned, he was fast discovering that he was weak. Weak and aroused, he amended with a groan as she shifted position, throwing one arm over his waist and one leg over his thighs.

As she snuggled against him, her small body seeking more of the warmth his offered, Steven clenched his jaw. Now he couldn't wake her up even if he wanted to. If she opened her eyes and found herself draped over him like this, she would be out of there so fast it would make his head spin. Of course it couldn't spin any faster than it was right now, he acknowledged sardonically as he breathed in the delicious scent of her hair.

Steven spent the next half hour in an agony of pleasure that was very close to pain. He could look his fill, but not touch. Feel, but not act on his feelings. He wanted her more than he'd ever wanted a woman in his life, but he wouldn't take her until she was ready.

*Dear God! Let it be soon!* his mind screamed as her hand dropped below his waist and her palm settled warmly between his thighs. This torture was more than any sane man would endure, but suddenly Steven realized he wasn't sane where she was concerned. He hadn't been himself since yesterday when he'd opened his eyes and been confronted with five feet of hostile, lovely, indignant, courageous femininity.

To his surprise, unlike any other woman he'd met, Samantha Charles was capable of touching off every one of his emotions. There had been moments in the past twenty-four hours when he'd been rocked to the depths of his soul by his conflicting feelings for her. As he recalled those moments, he was jolted by another realization.

He not only wanted to make love to her, he was falling in love with her!

"Chrisake, I just met the woman! How the hell did this happen?" Steven growled, totally forgetting that the woman in question was fast asleep on his chest. He remembered it when she moaned, and he knew that he would never forget it again as her palm closed warmly over him. "Samantha. You're killing me."

"Hmm?" Samantha responded to the raspy voice, though she wasn't aware who'd spoken until she opened her eyes. Once that occurred, she became aware of too many other things to ask for a repeat of what had been said.

"Oh, dear," she mumbled as she tried to convince her sluggish body to uncurl from its comfortable position. She was only marginally successful, but didn't understand why until she came more fully awake and realized that Steven was holding her in place. "What do you think you're doing?"

"I'm hugging you, dammit," Steven swore, tilting her chin up with his hand. "And now I'm going to kiss you. Want to make something of it?"

Samantha was shocked into complete wakefulness by the taut, belligerent look on his face. She began squirming, but as soon as she moved her hand, she realized how she'd wound up in this disturbing predicament. She felt the heated strength of his arousal against her palm, and her shock was replaced by embarrassment.

"I . . . I'm so sorry," she apologized, blushing profusely as she snatched her offending fingers away from him. "I . . . I didn't know what I was doing. Really, Steven. I had no idea. You should have stopped me . . . woken me up . . . something. . . ."

"Kindly shut up," Steven muttered gruffly, needing more than an apology to assuage the throbbing hunger in his body. "And if you want to make it off this couch, don't move!"

Samantha did what he said. She shut her mouth and went perfectly still, but the desire didn't lessen in his eyes. The longer he looked at her, the hotter his gaze became. Her own eyes then opened very wide, when at last he shook his head and announced, "I'm sorry, Samantha, but this isn't working. I'm afraid I still have to have that kiss."

She didn't argue. She'd planned to, but when she opened her mouth it was covered by his. The last thought she had before she stopped thinking was an excuse for his assault on her lips, an excuse as well as her surrender. After all, Steven was a virile man with only so much willpower, and she *had* pushed him over the edge. This was the inevitable result, she told herself, and they both had to share responsibility for it.

The kiss became kisses as Steven trailed his lips down her throat and around to a spot beneath her ear that was incredibly sensitive. Samantha shivered when he buried his mouth there, and she couldn't prevent a tiny moan of delight. After their last intimate encounter, she was embarrassed by the sound, but Steven seemed pleased. He slid his fingers into her hair and kissed her ear, murmuring soft sounds into it as he did so.

Samantha knew she should make him stop, at least make an attempt to move off him, but then he kissed her again, and she exchanged what she should do with what she wanted to do. Steven incited something wild and reckless in her, broke through the reserve that she'd built around herself since her divorce. She tasted him with a seductive rhythm that was all passionate woman, and his response was all man.

A long minute later, it was over. Groaning, Steven lifted her up and set her down on the other side of him. "You make it damned hard for me to do the right thing."

"The right thing?" Samantha mumbled in flustered confusion as she pushed a tangled length of hair out of her eyes. With growing consternation, she relived the past few minutes in her mind and realized what Steven must be thinking. She'd offered no resistance to his kisses. Indeed, toward the end, it was she who'd been the aggressor.

"You think I was throwing myself at you," she whispered harshly, totally humiliated. Steven had passed judgment on her when she was ten years old, and she'd just given him reason to believe that judgment was correct. "You think I'm easy! A dumb blond bimbo who'll go after anything in pants! That's why you pushed me away."

Steven drew in a ragged breath and waited for his heartbeat to slow down so he could formulate an appropriate response to her ridiculous accusation. Why she would think such a thing was beyond him, unless she'd heard something of his reputation. There had been a time in his younger days when he'd been attracted to dumb blondes, but a voluptuous body without brains no longer held any attraction for him. He would set her straight on that score right now.

"You're not a bimbo," he asserted firmly. "What you are is an exhausted mother of three active children who fell asleep and didn't realize what was happening until it was too late. You're also a very passionate and very loving lady, Samantha, and with your defenses down, it was easy for me to take advantage of you. But I don't want you turning to me in a vulnerable moment. When we make love for the first time, I want us both to be fully aware of what we're doing."

Steven assumed her silence was a condemnation of his presumption that they would eventually end up in the same bed. Knowing her stance on that prospect, he took her hand in both of his and pleaded, "Please don't use this lapse in judgment as an excuse to walk out on me... it's just that you're so damned beautiful... and I temporarily forgot the rules. You've accepted a job as my housekeeper, and I'll try my best not to ask anything more of you until you want there to be more."

Samantha could hardly believe her ears and was having difficulty assimilating what she'd heard. Steven didn't sound as if her wanton behavior had repulsed him. On the contrary, he made it sound as if he respected her as a lady...a beautiful lady and blamed himself for taking advantage of her in a weak moment. Was it possible that he truly felt that way?

"I knew what I was doing," she admitted, forcing herself to be honest, even when she would have liked to let him go on thinking he was solely responsible for what had just transpired between them. "And I'm just as guilty of breaking the rules."

Bemused by her honesty, Steven muttered under his breath, "Some rules are meant to be broken."

Lips twitching, Samantha pulled her hand out of his grasp. He really was an impossible man, but she found it difficult not to like him. "But you just said you'd do your best to abide by them," she reminded.

"I will," Steven promised with a sigh as he stood up from the couch. "Even though you're one terrific kisser."

"And I will, too," Samantha declared solemnly, then grinned up at him. "Even though you're not half-bad yourself."

Steven pushed his hands into the front pockets of his jeans so he wouldn't be tempted to grab her again. "Let's go up to bed," he suggested wickedly, but she knew it wasn't a serious proposition.

"To our separate rooms," Samantha agreed, her eyes dancing with laughter as he groaned in frustration.

* * *

Breakfast the next morning was a hurried affair. Steven was the last one downstairs, looking every inch the successful tycoon in a navy pin-striped suit. With a wistful look at the table, he said that he was running late and barely took time to gulp down a cup of coffee before he was out the door.

Feeling slightly wistful herself as she watched him climb into the Jeep and drive away, Samantha sat down and ate breakfast with the children. At least they had the time to compliment her on her culinary efforts this morning, and they also stuck around long enough to help her clean up after the meal. Once that was done, however, they took off for the living room and the VCR.

Samantha would have preferred that they do something more constructive with their time than watch movies on television, but having them occupied made it easier for her to dive into her work. By noon, she'd dusted, cleaned and vacuumed the most frequently used rooms on the first floor, except for Steven's study. The door to that room was closed, and though Samantha was curious to see what his private domain was like, she took the closed door as a directive to stay out.

After lunch, when the children were napping, she began on the bedrooms. As expected, all of them were beautifully decorated, if something of a mess. In one, she found Christmas wrapping paper, which told her exactly how long it had gone without a thorough cleaning. Two of the bedrooms had a masculine decor, one of which she assumed was Steven's brother

Robert's, but the closets were empty, telling her he was no longer in residence.

Samantha could understand why Steven would feel lonely at times. A large home like this was meant to house an equally large family. Delicious smells should emanate from that fabulous kitchen, and the sound of voices should echo up the wide stairs. The laughter of children and the noise of running feet should be heard up and down the long hallways. The house practically called out for people, Samantha thought as she passed from room to room and saw the family portraits and personal items, antiques and silly knickknacks that revealed how many of them had once resided here.

Yet today the firstborn son of the Armstrong dynasty lived alone. As she walked to the last bedroom at the end of the hall, Samantha thought about that and felt a strange hurt in the area around her heart. Steven had been born and raised to take care of money and things and people, but who took care of him?

As she entered the master bedroom, Samantha noted that it was exceedingly luxurious, but was also in the worst shape of the lot. Apparently, since there was no one else living in the house who might care, Steven saw no need to pick up after himself. The fact that he'd slept there was evidenced by the rumpled sheets on the huge four-poster bed, the pair of jeans and shirt on the floor next to it and the cowboy boots sticking out from beneath.

Even with all the personal items that proved the room was inhabited by a male, it had obviously been designed by a woman. Steven's mother, Samantha presumed as she viewed her spacious surroundings. Oh, yes, the woman had indeed had exquisite taste.

The creamy white walls were offset by an ornate oval mirror, picturesque landscape paintings in gilt frames, and pretty rose-pink drapes that were drawn back from the three huge windows. The small sitting area held pink, satin-covered chairs, a low glass-topped table and an antique chaise lounge, which Steven used as a laundry basket. The floor was covered by rich, eggshell-blue carpeting with a beautifully designed border highlighted in rose and beige. Samantha refused to think about how much she would enjoy occupying the room, or what it might be like to share it with Steven.

Intent on her housekeeping chores, she marched into the adjoining bathroom, which was even more impressive than the bedroom. The pedestal sink and large tub were blue-gray marble, and the fixtures were gold! For those who didn't want to take a bath, there was a glass-enclosed shower with three shower heads that sprayed in separate directions.

Samantha thought about the dinky bathroom in her house, the tiny shower stall with the plastic curtain surrounding a central floor drain. As she turned on the water in Steven's shower and began to wipe down the marble tiles, she thought about the leaky washers in her sink and the sporadic water pressure in her shower that could spurt either cold or hot on a whim.

Oh, what she wouldn't give for a leisurely bath, to soak in fragrant bubbles with hot water up to her chin. Recalling the perfectly adequate white claw tub in the bathroom assigned to her and the children, Samantha took a quick glance at her watch, and decided to take a break. The children wouldn't wake up for another half hour or so, which wouldn't give her that much time to linger in the tub, but it would have to do. Besides, she assured herself happily, a half hour in the tub was better than a five-minute shower any day of the week. And for the amount of work she'd already put in today, she felt she deserved a reward.

At the same time Samantha was luxuriating in her bath, Steven was cutting short his last meeting in town. He could trade information with the other members of the Cattleman's Association any time, but he didn't know how long he had with Samantha before she figured out that he'd lied about ordering her a new furnace. Once she knew that, she would take it upon herself to make the arrangements, and he would have to tell her the truth about who owned her house and land. By the time that happened, he hoped she would be just as enamored of him as he was of her.

If not, he knew he would be in for a very hard time, but whether Samantha liked it or not, she wasn't going back to that run-down old place. She would be furious when she realized that option was closed to her, but he could live with that. He didn't want her to hate him, but he couldn't allow her and the children to continue chasing a pipe dream that could only lead them to starvation. He already cared about them too much to allow that, and since they were living on his land, he felt responsible, unlike the man who should have shouldered some responsibility for their welfare.

Every time Steven thought about that selfish bastard Samantha had married, he felt the urge to kill. It hadn't been that difficult to figure out what had happened, and after a few phone calls, Steven's worst suspicions had been confirmed. According to his past employer and the lawyer who'd handled Samantha's divorce, Bradley Charles had skipped out of town with another woman, leaving his wife and three children without any means of financial support.

Steven knew Samantha had good reason to mistrust his sex, but he was going to do his best to make her trust him. Whatever it took to break down the barriers she'd erected against him and win her heart, he was prepared to do it, for even though he was still having trouble believing it, the fact of the matter was that she and her children had already won his.

If nothing else, the past few months had taught him that he wasn't cut out to live alone. By the time a man reached his mid-thirties, he needed a family, a wife and children to share his life with. As far as Steven was concerned, the kindly Fates had decided to step in when it became obvious that if it were left up to him, he would end up single. Instead he'd been presented with a ready-made family, and all he had to do was devote himself to keeping them.

For the past several years, he hadn't allotted much time to the pursuit of women, and the ones he'd ended up catching without putting forth any effort, he hadn't wanted. But Samantha Charles was a different story. He definitely wanted her, and he was willing to dedicate all of his energies to catching her.

With that goal in mind, Steven left his office much earlier than usual and arrived back at the ranch before the sun went down. The sight that greeted him when he opened the back door produced a huge lump in his throat, and he came to a complete stop before anyone noticed his arrival. He couldn't have imagined a more cozy domestic scene, or one that fit his fantasies more perfectly.

Samantha was removing a delicious-smelling roast from the oven, her cheeks flushed a lovely pink from the heat. She wasn't wearing any makeup, but in the golden light of sunset, her complexion glowed, and her blond hair looked like a halo. She'd pulled it up in a topknot and tied it with a pale blue ribbon, but several wispy tendrils had escaped their confinement and were curled prettily at her nape. She was even wearing a frilly apron that had belonged to his mother over her blue jeans and blouse.

The children presented an equally delightful picture. Heather had a dish towel tied around her waist and was standing on a stool, busily cooking an imaginary meal in the empty pots that stood on the kitchen counter. Zack and Tony were setting the round oak table, and haranguing each other over the proper placement of silverware.

"Hi, fellas," Steven greeted with a wide grin as he stepped over the threshold. "Something sure smells good."

"We're having pot roast," Zack announced, licking his lips. "With plenty of mashed potatoes and gravy."

"And scalloped corn," Tony added, since the vegetable dish was his personal favorite.

"And chocolate cream pie!" Heather exclaimed happily from the other side of the room.

"Looks like your mom has been busy," Steven said, loosening his tie as he walked past the stove. "And that's great, because I'm starving.

"And I especially like chocolate cream pie," he confided to Heather.

Samantha was stirring away, but she glanced up at him with a relieved smile. "I'm glad to hear that. I wasn't sure what you like, but you said you were a meat-and-potatoes man, so I thought I'd stick with some old standbys."

"You thought right," Steven complimented as he walked through the swinging door into the dining room. "And I'll be ready to dig in as soon as I change out of this suit."

With a deep sense of contentment, Steven began to whistle as he headed for the stairs, but he stopped abruptly when his brain finally registered something his eyes had been slow to report. "Couldn't be," he said as he walked back into the dining room and saw that what couldn't be, definitely was.

"So much for that fantasy!" he muttered darkly. At the far end of the long, polished mahogany table was a place setting for one. Obviously employers were not expected to dine with the hired help and he wasn't to be included in that cozy, family setup in the kitchen.

"Well, we'll see about that, lady," he growled as he yanked off his suit coat and resumed his walk to the stairs. "We'll just see about that!"

# Seven

It was past midnight, but Samantha couldn't sleep so she slipped on her robe over her pink flannel nightgown and went down to the kitchen to make herself some hot chocolate. She knew what was causing her insomnia, but didn't know what to do about it. Therefore, she intended to soothe herself with a warm drink, just as she'd done for the past three out of four nights. Besides, the only time she really had to be alone with her thoughts was when the children were tucked in for the night and Steven went up to his room.

Considering the events of the past week, she had quite a lot to think about, but to her self-disgust, her thoughts were mainly centered around sex. She seemed to be obsessed by them. And according to her current state of agitation, she realized that she couldn't go on like this much longer. Lack of sleep was definitely taking its toll, and she was becoming a very cranky person.

A cranky person who had only herself to blame for the sorry shape she was in. No, Samantha reevaluated that judgment, she could also blame a certain Prince Charming look-alike named Steven Armstrong. It was Steven who was trying to ride in on his white charger and make her forget all the harsh lessons she'd learned since growing up. Thus far, he was doing a great job of trampling all over her peace of mind, riding rough-shod over her better judgment.

Steven wanted to take care of her, but she'd fallen into that trap already and look where it had gotten her? The best thing a woman could do for herself was learn to stand on her own two feet. She'd learned that lesson the hard way, after discovering that the man who'd promised to provide for her had feet of clay. Yet, even knowing what the consequences might be, she was still having a difficult time keeping herself from placing the new man in her life up on a pedestal.

"It's just that he's being so blasted nice," Samantha said as she tore open a packet of instant cocoa and poured it into her mug.

Because of Steven, the past several days had been some of the happiest in her life. Because of him, her children were warm, happy and well fed, her sick cattle were on the mend, and her new furnace was on order. The heating company had informed Steven that the unit required was an off size that had to be specially modified by the manufacturer, so it might take several weeks for it to arrive, but Samantha was less upset about that lengthy delay than she would have been a week ago. The longer she worked for Steven, the more able she would be to pay for the large expenditure without having to apply for additional credit—credit she knew would be denied her.

Now if only she could figure out if the man who was responsible for all these pleasant benefits had ulterior motives. Was Steven just being a Good Samaritan, or was there another purpose behind his kindness? Sometimes she got the distinct impression that he knew something concerning her that she didn't know, and wouldn't like if she did—but how could that be possible?

She hadn't been anywhere near him for almost ten years. Of course he spent a lot of time at his office in Billings, and she and Brad had lived there, but they certainly hadn't traveled in the same circles. No, Samantha told herself, the funny feeling she had that something was wrong was as silly as her assumption that Steven would be next to impossible to work for.

As it had turned out, he was not only the best looking, but the nicest boss she'd ever had. Although she was the employee, and he the employer, it didn't seem that way. Since the first meal she'd prepared as his housekeeper, Steven had effectively demolished her notion that she and the children must keep to their proper place. Instead of taking his meal in the dining room, he'd brought his dishes back out to the kitchen table, plunked himself down on a chair and announced that from then on, they would all eat together.

To Samantha's astonishment, instead of being pleased by the preferential treatment she'd thought to afford him as her employer, he'd actually seemed hurt by being banished to the dining room. When Samantha had explained that she'd assumed that he would prefer to eat dinner in a more formal setting, she'd been told in no uncertain terms that she'd assumed wrong. As long as they were staying in his house, he would be taking his meals with them, thank you very much. He was a very confusing man.

In the days since that incident, Samantha had been forced to reevaluate several other notions she had about men in general and Steven in particular. For one thing, not all men were completely self-centered. Steven went out of his way to make time for the children, and he rarely lost patience with them, no matter how busy he was or how badly they behaved. He was firm in his dealings with them, but he never spoke to them in anger. Even when Zack had pulled down a rifle from the gun case and aimed it at Tony, Steven hadn't overreacted. Instead he'd calmly pointed out the dangers of playing with guns and given all three children an instructive course in firearm safety.

Afterward he'd apologized to Samantha for neglecting to keep the gun case locked, even going so far as to call himself an idiot for not remembering what a temptation that antique collection was to a small boy. Brad had done things twice as stupid during their marriage, but not once had he ever apologized or even hinted that he might have been wrong. To Brad, admitting an error was an admission of weakness, but it was obvious that Steven didn't feel that way. His masculinity wasn't threatened by acknowledging his human failings, and in Samantha's mind, that made him the stronger of the two.

In every way she could think of, Steven was stronger, much more of a man than Brad ever had been or could ever hope to be. Oh, Steven could be arrogant at times and extremely irritating, but the longer she knew him, the more she came to understand that he was also capable of great tenderness and compassion. Neither trait was one she'd thought to credit him with a week ago.

To Samantha's amusement, the first day or two he'd handled Heather as if her bones were made of glass. But then when the little girl had cried at being excluded from the roughhousing he enjoyed with the boys after supper each night, he'd immediately tumbled her right down on the rug and pretended to wrestle her as if she were a worthy opponent. He'd even allowed her to pummel his chest and pull on his hair, before he'd growled like an enraged grizzly and tossed her up into the air until she was squealing with laughter. The child had adored him ever since.

Actually all three of her children adored him, and Samantha was fast surrendering to the same emotion. It was incredible how easily he got through her defenses and made her aware that she was a woman who'd gone too long without the admiration of a man. The way he smiled at her made her feel special, and when his dark eyes looked at her in a certain way, her entire body grew warm with desire. It had reached the point where all he had to do was walk into the room, and she experienced the most disturbing palpitations.

And Samantha knew he was well aware of the effect he had on her. Not only was he aware, but he took outrageous advantage of it. He couldn't walk past her without some part of his body accidentally brushing against her, or talk to her without standing too close. He gazed longingly at her lips, but never tried to make a pass at her, and this was frustrating Samantha so badly she was almost ready to make one at him.

"Which is exactly what that sexy devil wants," Samantha groaned out loud as she placed her mug inside the microwave and slammed the door shut. "Well, I've got my pride, and I refuse to throw myself at him. I've done that enough times as it is."

"Like hell."

Samantha whirled around to find Steven lounging against the door frame. "And if you don't throw yourself at him again soon, the poor devil is going to go straight out of his sexy mind."

"You were eavesdropping!" Samantha accused, her mouth going dry as her eyes registered what he was wearing—nothing but a pair of faded jeans that rode dangerously low on his lean hips and were so worn that his potent masculinity was visible to anyone who cared to look.

Steven tried to appear grossly offended by her accusation, but his grin spoiled the effect. He saw the difficulty she was having keeping her eyes above his waist, and he was pleased as punch about it. "It's the middle of the night, Samantha. If we had company, I'd plead guilty to that, but you were talking to yourself. How was I to know it was a private conversation?"

Samantha sputtered over his logic, which made him laugh. "It's not as if you were telling me something I don't already know, and since you're as frustrated as I am, I'd think you'd be glad that we've finally got this out into the open. Now maybe we can do something about it."

"If you think I'm going to...that I'll..." Samantha started, then stopped, her cheeks flushed with embarrassment. "You know what I mean."

Steven nodded, his dark eyes caressing her brushed flannel robe. She looked so much better in it than he had. Even in a worn-out robe and floppy slippers, her blond hair messed and her features devoid of make-up, she was the loveliest woman he'd ever seen. "Unfortunately I know exactly what you mean, and that's why we need to talk. I'm as close to the breaking point as you are."

Upon hearing that, Samantha decided that what she needed wasn't talk, but distance. Taking her hot chocolate out of the microwave, she walked over to the kitchen table and sat down. "I won't have an affair with you. You may think I'm like that, but I'm not. I don't sleep around."

Steven glared at her. He hated it when she made comments like that, as if she assumed he thought of her as some kind of a loose woman. "I know you don't."

Going to the cupboard, he took down a mug for himself, going through the same motions she had earlier. He glanced over at her, but she was staring intently at the pattern on the tablecloth, unwilling to look at him. Leaning back against the counter, he said, "Do you consider me a friend, Samantha?"

The unexpected question brought up her head. "A... a friend?"

"Well, I guess that answers that." Steven's shoulders slumped in defeat. For a week now, he'd been bending over backward to get her to like him, to trust him, and it was obvious that she hadn't even contemplated the idea of friendship with him. They could hardly move to the next step if she hadn't taken the first one, and he didn't know if he had the perseverance to wait any longer for her to catch up.

"Maybe you don't know what a friend is," he said in annoyance.

Samantha gaped at him over the rim of her mug. Was that pain she saw in his eyes? "Of course, I do," she declared tartly, unsure where this conversation was heading. As far as she was concerned, being friends with him was the least of her worries. It was thoughts of being his lover that absorbed all her waking hours, fast turning her into a chronic insomniac.

Cleaning his bedroom had become sheer torture for her. Each time she made his bed, she imagined them in it. They were both naked, their limbs tangled together in the sheets. She would be writhing beneath the powerful length of his body, her mouth yielding eagerly to his insistent lips. Then when the pleasure became too much to bear, she would arch her back and he would thrust into her, and—

"So, tell me," Steven prompted in exasperation when he saw that her attention wasn't on him, but on the tiny yellow daisies in the wallpaper. "If you're through counting flowers, how do you define a friend?''

With a guilty jerk, Samantha jumped out of his four-poster bed and back into reality. "A friend?" she exclaimed, forcing her brain to switch gears. "Okay... a friend is someone you can count on when you're in trouble, someone who'll listen to you and understand your feelings, a person who likes you for who you are on the inside."

Steven took the chair opposite hers, striving for patience. "This last week, I think I've proved that you can count on me, Samantha, and I like everything about you, inside and out. I think you like me, too. Doesn't that mean we've got the basis for a solid friendship here?" he asked quietly, watching her face as his words sunk in. She looked so stunned it made him lose his temper.

"Why is that idea so damned inconceivable to you?" he demanded. "What in hell have you got against me!"

Shocked by his anger, Samantha almost choked on a swallow of her hot chocolate. "I... I don't have anything against you."

"All I want is to be your friend. Is that so much to ask?"

"Well, no... but—"

"But what!"

Samantha didn't like being yelled at, so she yelled back, "But that's not all you want!"

"Yes, it is!"

"Oh, no, it's not," Samantha retorted, becoming more furious by the second. Who did he think he was trying to kid? Standing up from her chair, she spat, "Do you think I'm an idiot? Not more than five minutes ago, you admitted that what you really want is to make love to me!"

Steven slammed his empty mug down on the table and stood up to face her. The hell with patience, enough was enough. "Damned right I do!"

"Then why the dickens don't you?" she challenged, blue eyes flashing.

Incredulous, Steven stared at her, but when she attempted to walk past him, he grabbed her arm and pulled her up against him. "If that's what you want, I'd be happy to oblige!"

As soon as her palms made contact with his bare chest, Samantha lost all her fight. "That's what I want," she informed him miserably, tears welling up beneath her lids. "And that's why I'm so upset, because I won't be able to live with myself if I do."

Steven closed his eyes and tried to get a grip on the rampaging passion that surged through his body. One of these days, this damned changeable woman was going to give him a heart attack. Keeping up with her moods was causing him acute mental stress, and at the moment, severe physical pain. One second she was all womanly challenge demanding his passion, and the next she was a hurt child needing comfort. And, to the detriment of his nervous system, he was never prepared when the switch took place.

When it came to women, he was normally the one who left them guessing, but the shoe was on the other foot with Samantha. Half the time he had no idea what she was thinking, and the other half, he didn't want to know. If Rob or Conlan had been here to watch him run rings around himself in order to please her, they would have laughed themselves silly.

After several tense seconds, Steven finally felt he could touch her as a friend instead of as a lover. He cupped her head in his hand and pressed down so her cheek was resting on his chest. "Samantha, you're being much too hard on yourself. What you feel for me isn't wrong. It's very, very right."

"Hmmph." Samantha's less-than-positive response to that was muffled against his left shoulder.

Steven's muscles tightened as he absorbed her jab to his ego. "There's something special going on between us," he insisted stubbornly. "And I think we owe it to ourselves to find out what it is and how far it's going to take us."

Samantha swiveled her head to throw off his palm, her breath catching as her cheek rubbed across his hard, smooth flesh. As if jolted by an electrical charge, her fingers tingled with the need to touch more of him, and she wrapped her arms around his waist. She was standing so close that she could feel his muscles ripple whenever he moved, feel the strength of his heart-beat, the warmth of his breath against her hair.

"I know what's going on between us," she sighed in resignation, surrendering to what she knew was wrong, but also inevitable. It felt so good to be in his arms. "It's plain, old-fashioned lust, and if you're not careful, it's going to take us right into the nearest bedroom."

Even as she spoke, her fingers caressed him, glided up and down his naked spine. Beneath the flannel layer of her nightclothes, he could feel her full breasts respond to each rise and fall of his chest. "It's not just lust, dammit," he swore, groaning as her fingers probed beneath the waistband of his jeans. "And how in hell can I be careful with your hands on me like that?"

"You can't," Samantha breathed, so hungry for him that she no longer cared about anything but the need to satisfy that hunger. "And I can't either. I'm just not strong enough."

Her hands moved down the back of his jeans. "Samantha!"

"It's all right, Steven," she whispered. She wanted him so badly, and she couldn't stop the wanting no matter how hard she tried. She began kissing his chest, tasting him with her lips, breathing in his marvelous scent, and she couldn't get enough.

Close to losing control, Steven lifted her head to face him. "Are you saying what I think you are? Feeling what I'm feeling?"

Samantha looked into his eyes and saw her own passion reflected back to her. "All I know is that I want to make love with you, Steven. Tonight."

"And you're not going to change your mind again?" Steven asked, watching her uplifted face, seeing her lips part. God, how he wanted that soft mouth. For days and days now he'd wanted it. "Because I think it will kill me if you do."

"I won't change my mind," she promised, though a flicker of guilt worked its way through the waves of passion clouding her mind. "But the children can't—"

"They won't," Steven vowed, scooping her up in his arms before she could finish her sentence. "I don't want to hurt them any more than you do. We'll be very discreet."

True to his word, Steven carried her to the back stairs, which led to the hallway in front of the master suite. When he reached the upstairs landing, he stopped to make sure all was quiet at the other end of the hall before he opened the door to his room and carried her inside. But, once the door was closed behind them, all discretion was cast aside.

"It seems like I've waited forever for this," he murmured hoarsely as he laid her down on his bed. Even before he lay down beside her, she was reaching for him, but he stepped out of reach. He wanted their lovemaking to be slow, because if he didn't stay in control, he would take her with a ruthless hunger, and she would never let him near her again.

Standing at the side of the bed, he stripped off his jeans, and Samantha watched, completely entranced. Not in her entire life had she seen a more beautiful male body. In the silvery light of the moon, Steven was magnificent. No wonder women had been clamoring for his attention since he had been a teenager. They would have done so even if he wasn't an eligible bachelor and the richest man in six counties.

Samantha could barely breathe as she gazed at him and saw how much he wanted her. Soon she would know what it was like to be made love to by him. At last the fantasies that awakened her at night and haunted her during the day would become reality. The thought made her tremble, and she pleaded, "Hurry, Steven. Please hurry."

Steven joined her on the bed with a groan from deep in his chest. He kissed her as if he were never going to stop; gentle kisses, fiery kisses, kisses that stole her breath away and touched her very soul. His mouth blazed a path down her throat, until his lips encountered the tiny buttons of her nightgown, and then his fingers were there to uncover what his mouth sought so eagerly. "Do you have any idea how sexy this thing is?" he whispered.

Samantha bit her lips as she felt her nightgown removed by impatient hands, but his touch immediately gentled when she was naked. "I knew you'd look like this," he murmured. "I've known since that first night when I ran into you and we fell down in the snowbank. Even under that thick coat, I could tell how tiny you were, how beautifully and delicately made."

Samantha's eyes widened. "That's what you were thinking!"

Steven grinned, delighted by her shock. "But I wasn't prepared for these gorgeous breasts," he teased, cupping her fullness in his palm. "I didn't realize you had these lovely curves until we got in the house and you took off your coat. Was that ever a pleasant surprise."

"You were...were..."

"I sure was," Steven agreed huskily as he lowered his head. "And I couldn't wait to do this."

His tongue flicked a hardened nipple, teasing and tasting, while her other breast was softly cradled in his hand. Samantha couldn't lie still beneath his fire-edged kisses. His caressing fingers sent sparkles of heat and shivers of passion through her. They'd barely begun, yet she was already more excited and aroused than she'd ever been in her life.

"I can't wait, either." Lacing her fingers through his thick hair, Samantha kissed his neck and solid shoulders. Running her hand along his chest, she caressed the dark curls of hair down to his belly while he explored the mysteries of her body with his lips.

As his mouth returned to hers, Samantha answered the demand of his lips by opening to him, meeting the challenge of his invading tongue, tasting him as he tasted her. All of her senses cried out with the same incredible message. She'd thought herself in love before, but this was love. She was in love with Steven. No matter how much she fought against it, she could deny the truth no longer. His touch, the mere sight of him, excited her, but there was more, so much more.

If only he could love her, too, but Samantha knew that if-onlys rarely happened. Steven liked her and desired her body, which made her good enough for a blazing affair, but not marriage. The firstborn son of the Armstrong dynasty would never consider marriage to a little nobody like her.

She had to remember that things like that only happened in fairy tales. Steven may have swept her off her feet like Prince Charming, but this Cinderella came with three children. He might feel the urge to carry her away, but he'd soon realize the impossibility of that feat. All five of them would never fit on his white charger.

Attuned to her slightest movement, Steven felt the anxiety in her, but mistook the cause. For him, making love to her was an expression of his love and commitment, but she had no way of knowing the depth of his feelings, and it was much too soon to tell her. The last man in her life had taught her that she couldn't trust in the forever kind of love, but no matter how long it took, Steven meant to teach her otherwise. She was so special, a beautiful woman who deserved that very special and lasting kind of emotion.

"Don't worry, Samantha," he whispered soothingly. He reached into the top drawer of the nightstand, knowing she was worrying about protection. "All you have to do is put your arms around me, I'll take care of the rest."

He didn't give her time to argue. His palm slid between her thighs too fast, too expertly, claiming the very core of her.

She wrapped her arms around him because it was the only thing she could do as he drove inside her. As fast as he claimed her, he made her understand that for these precious moments, her emotions belonged to him as much as her body did. Every part of her was his, as was the passion that surged in and around her, in and around him.

Steven's control shattered as she climaxed, and his instincts took over. Sheathed in her warmth, he drove into her again and again, and she counteracted every one of his thrusts. As he plunged over the edge of reason, he whispered, "You're my woman...Samantha...mine."

* * *

As the early-morning sunlight filtered into the room, Samantha slid silently out of bed. After replacing her nightgown and robe, she looked back to where Steven was lying relaxed and asleep after a night of love. And it had been love, at least on her part. As she crept out of the room, she tried desperately to convince herself that Steven felt the same way. There had been too much emotion behind every caress he made, every word he spoke, for it to have been mere lust. Yet, not once during the night had he admitted to feeling more than desire for her.

"Not once," she repeated to herself as she passed through her bedroom and into the adjoining bath. "Not once."

The tears came as she stood beneath the hot spray of the shower. The truth was painful, but it had to be faced. Steven's love for her was restricted to the confines of his bed, and she would be a fool to believe otherwise. Unfortunately for her, their passionate joining had only sharpened the agony of knowing she could be his woman, but never his wife.

Last night she had let down all the barriers she'd erected against him, but today, if she wanted to survive, she would have to do some rebuilding. She knew that as long as she stayed in this house, there could be no going back to a platonic relationship, but the next time they made love, she had to protect her heart.

Next time she would give him all of her passion, but keep her soul to herself. She might be obsessed by his touch, greedy with need for his possession, but she wouldn't reveal her desperation for his love. She was a realist, and realists understood that fairy tales never came true. "I'm having a flaming, passionate affair with a rich, gorgeous, sexy man," she announced to the gleaming white tiles on the shower walls. "But that's as far as it goes."

As she placed her head under the hard spray and began washing her hair, she was unable to hear the despairing edge to her voice as she vowed, "And I'm going to enjoy it while it lasts."

# Eight

Y ou must have gotten up bright and early this morning, Samantha. This is quite some feast," Steven said as he joined the children who were already seated at the kitchen table. He didn't know what to put on his plate first, the honey-cured ham and scrambled eggs, French toast and maple syrup, or the piping hot baking soda biscuits and creamed gravy.

With a heart-stopping grin, he eyed the diminutive woman standing by the stove, loving the way she looked in his kitchen. Actually he loved the way she looked everywhere, he admitted, his eyes gleaming with the recollection of how she'd looked last night after several rounds of lovemaking. The only thing that would have made that memory better was if he'd woken up this morning and found her still lying beside him.

But that day would come, he assured himself. Last night had proven to him that their being together on a permanent basis was inevitable. At long last he'd found the woman who was to be his wife.

Samantha saw the way Steven was staring at her and was afraid he might say or do something so revealing that the children would start asking embarrassing questions like, "Are you going to be our new daddy?" Steven would make a wonderful father, but where her children were concerned that just wasn't in the cards. "Who needs more orange juice?" she inquired, hoping to break the sensual pull of a pair of dark eyes.

Thankfully Zack took her up on her offer, and she was able to turn away from Steven as she refilled her son's glass. Her relief was short-lived, however, for as soon as she was finished pouring Zack's orange juice, Steven was holding up his glass. Her fingers shook slightly as she tipped the pitcher, and she almost dropped it into Steven's lap when he said, "If I didn't know you'd already discovered a much better way of getting there, I'd say you were trying to get to my heart through my stomach."

Knowing the way he was referring to, Samantha blushed, and she felt her knees giving out. She quickly took her own seat at the table. "It's Saturday, and Chuck told me that you usually put in some long days on the weekend. I thought you might need the extra calories."

"Nope." At the same time as Steven negated that assumption, he piled his plate high with the food she'd prepared. "I worked hard all week, so I'm taking the day off to go fishing."

"Fishing!" Four voices chorused at once, but Heather was the first to take it one step further. "Can we come, Steben? Can we? Can we?"

"We're all going, first thing after breakfast," Steven said, putting all three of the children out of their misery. A second later he cleared his throat and looked up at Samantha with a guilty expression on his face. "That is, if it's okay with your mother."

Samantha smiled. It came slowly, but the man was learning. "Do fish bite this early in the season?"

"Sure," both twins exclaimed at once, though neither of them had ever been fishing, so they didn't have any idea what they were talking about.

Steven, on the other hand, offered knowledgeably, "Trout prefer cold water. Now that the snow's melted, the streams will be running fast, and those trout will be biting."

"I haven't been fishing since I was a kid. I hope I can remember how to bait a hook," Samantha said, and her words were quickly followed by a round of enthusiastic applause from the children.

"She's letting us!" Zack exclaimed as if he were truly amazed.

"Of course I am. It sounds like fun," Samantha said, wondering how long her children had held the opinion that she was such a wet blanket.

Knowing what she was thinking, Steven winked at her. "It *will* be fun," he guaranteed. "I know of a special fishing hole where all the big ones live, and I've gotta mind to catch myself the biggest granddaddy of 'em all."

"I've gotta mind to, too," Zack declared firmly while attempting to fill his mouth with more food than would possibly fit. Scowling over at his brother, he ordered, "Clean your plate, Tony. You know Mom won't let us go unless we eat every bite, and hurry up, will ya?"

"I'm hurrying," Tony said as he took another bite of his French toast. "But she won't let us go till the dishes are washed anyways."

Zack hopped up from the table and dashed for the utility closet. "It had ta be my day for garbage," he complained as he tugged the black plastic bag out of the tall metal can. "I hate hauling garbage."

"First we work, then we play," Heather quoted in a tone of voice so much like her mother's that Samantha winced. Now she understood how the kids had gotten the impression that she was all work and no play. She glanced across the table at Steven to see where he stood on this subject, almost certain whose side he would be on.

Steven had enough wealth to be able to play whenever he wanted and hire someone else to do the work, but she and her children would never be in that position. To be fair, Samantha had to admit that Steven worked hard, extremely hard, but his dedication to his business didn't spring from the same source as her dedication to a job. Even owning her own place hadn't diminished the necessity of keeping her nose to the grindstone. Steven, on the other hand, worked because he wanted to, not because he had to.

Aware of her eyes on him, Steven said, "Your mother's right, kids. How can we have any fun if we've got all these chores waiting for us when we get home?''

Tony was the first to see the wisdom behind this rationale. ''Yeah? And it's not fair for Mom to have to do it all when we get back.''

''Is too. She's the housekeeper, not us,'' Zack argued, unaware of the effect his words had on his mother. ''We shouldn't have to do nothin'.''

Samantha felt as if she'd just been punched in the stomach. What Zack said was true. She was the housekeeper, and all household chores should fall to her, but she'd kept up the routines the children followed at home so they wouldn't forget what responsibilities she expected them to carry. After hearing Zack talk, she could see that for all her good intentions, one of her children was already living in a dream world. Why hadn't she taken this possibility into account when she'd accepted this job?

All three of her children were too young to understand that just because they were allowed to enjoy all the luxuries available at the Triple A, this life-style wouldn't be theirs on a permanent basis. As soon as the new furnace was installed, they were going back to a place that didn't have video games and big-screen television, or a heated pool, or horses to ride. Samantha could see now that they were going to have a very difficult adjustment to make when they returned home, and the longer the delay, the more difficult it would be.

It was about time she faced facts. A woman like herself didn't have long, passionate love affairs with handsome millionaires. What she had going here was a brief fling that could very well cause long-lasting emotional damage to her children. She could tell herself otherwise as often as she liked, but that was the ugly truth of the matter.

Unfortunately, after last night, her desire for Steven was like a rampaging fever that soared higher and higher whenever he came near her. *So leave,* Samantha ordered herself. *Get out before your fevered brain forgets the consequences of staying.*

Steven could almost see Samantha's brain working, and according to her stricken expression, her thoughts didn't fit in very well with his plans for their future. Without meaning to, Zack had revealed a serious problem his mother was going to have with him if she attempted to take him back to that miserable cabin. Ever since their arrival at the Triple A, the children had been having the time of their lives, and Steven had had the time of his, spoiling them rotten. He would never have done it if he'd known that it would curtail the amount of time he had to convince Samantha that she didn't want to go back there, either.

If it were possible, she would be on her way right now. He could read that intention in her eyes, and it terrified him. Afraid of the harm it might be doing to her children, she was prepared to sacrifice her relationship with him. If he wanted her to stay, he had to talk fast.

"Every man, woman and child who lives on a ranch has to do their share of chores, Zack. It takes a lot of work to keep this place running, and the only way we'll succeed is if we all pull together," Steven said, trying hard not to take his anxiety out on a six-year-old. "It doesn't matter who's been hired to do what, as long as the work gets done."

"I'm helping," Zack said, breathing hard as he dragged the garbage bag toward the back door.

Steven smiled approvingly. "Both your mother and I appreciate it, son. If I couldn't rely on Chuck and the boys to do some of my work today, and your mom couldn't rely on you guys to help out with these chores, we'd have to stay home instead of going fishing."

"I'll stack the dishes," Tony volunteered solemnly.

With a resigned shrug of her small shoulders, Heather sighed. "And I'll feed the kitties."

Samantha's lips twitched as she watched her daughter hop down from her chair and trudge toward the wicker basket that was placed near the back stairs. "Thanks, Steven," she murmured softly as Tony carried several plates to the sink. "I couldn't have said it any better myself."

Steven placed his hand down over hers and gazed deeply into her eyes. "You can't go home yet, Samantha. The snow's gone, but it's still plenty cold at night."

"I know," Samantha replied, continually amazed by Steven's ability to read her mind. "Just as you know that we'll be leaving as soon as it warms up, whether or not the furnace has arrived."

"Yes," Steven acknowledged harshly, making his decision. Today would have to be the day.

Steven's special fishing hole was located in an isolated ravine about twenty miles away from the ranch house. Even though they'd gone by Jeep, the trip took almost an hour, for the old logging trail they drove on was steep, winding and full of ruts. Even so, Samantha felt that every spine-jolting mile was worth it. The mountains were filled with lovely places, but this one was particularly beautiful.

To get to the rushing stream, they had to walk through a carpet of colorful wildflowers and duck beneath the fragrant branches of green spruce. Sunshine beamed off the huge wet granite boulders on each side of the ravine, making rainbows of mist above the clear water. And off in the distance, in every direction were the mighty Rockies, summit after summit of snowcapped magnificence.

There was a definite nip in the air, but it was offset by a warm breeze that made it possible for them to discard their heavy coats in favor of light jackets. After a five-minute walk, they rounded a steep cliff and arrived at a place where the stream tumbled over a waterfall and widened into a deep pool. Surrounding the pool were more spruce trees and a sprinkling of silver birch, patches of green grass and flat-topped rocks that would make perfect benches. It was an idyllic spot, a haven of peace and tranquility, completely cut off from the rest of the world.

"How on earth did you ever find this place?" Samantha asked Steven, who was passing out bamboo poles to everyone.

"I've made it my business to know every inch of Triple A land," Steven told her as he escorted a trio of pint-size fishermen to the edge of the pool and helped them cast their lines out into the water. "Sometimes a man needs to get away by himself for a while. This spot is at the northernmost edge of our land, the farthest away I could get from the house without actually leaving the property. There was a time when I used to come up here a lot."

His answer only inspired more questions in Samantha, but they weren't free to talk for the next hour. One after another the white and red bobbers went down, and both she and Steven had their hands full trying to keep up with three gleeful anglers. Tony wouldn't touch a worm, so every time he caught a fish, Steven had to rebait his hook, and Samantha had to untangle fishing line from tree limbs and bushes each time Heather swung her rod toward the water. As for Zack, he adored fishing and ended up landing the biggest catch of the day.

"Samantha! Come here and help me!" Steven howled. "Ouch! Dammit! Don't pull on your line, Zack!"

Samantha ran to where Steven was standing, fighting laughter when she saw that he was clutching the seat of his pants. Going down on one knee, she worked quickly to unsnag the hook from the denim, but that material wasn't all that was snagged. A highly embarrassed Steven had to drop his pants so she could dislodge the hook from his briefs as well.

Attempting to hide her grin, Samantha turned to Steven. "Did you bring a first aid kit? It's only a scratch, but considering where that hook had been we should really put some antiseptic on it."

"Now, you show some compassion," Steven growled. This day was not going at all according to plan. "Only after you half killed me."

Samantha's grin turned into an all-out laugh. "Yes ... well, I'm sure the wound is heinous, but I'm equally positive your poor...eh...posterior will make a speedy recovery, especially if you let me put some antiseptic on it."

Unused to being laughed at, Steven jerked his jeans up over his hips and stalked away toward the grass where he'd left the picnic basket. "Forget it, lady. You're not touching my poor posterior ever again."

Lips twitching, Samantha followed closely behind him. As Steven bent over to spread out a blanket, she gave his rear a gentle pat. With a provocative gleam in her eyes, she teased, "Not ever?"

Steven was about to retract his hasty words by dragging her down on the blanket, but as soon as the kids saw Samantha drop to her knees and open the picnic basket they came out of the bushes on a dead run. "Maybe sometime," he conceded, stepping to one side before getting trampled. With a sigh of frustration, he added, "But, unfortunately, not now."

"Looks like they've worked up quite a big appetite," Samantha said as sandwich wrappers went flying.

Steven's dark eyes sparkled with promise as he gazed down at her smiling face. "Not as big as mine."

Samantha reached into the basket, deliberately misinterpreting his statement. "Then you're in luck. Here's a sandwich with your name on it."

Steven dropped down beside her. "Now if I were really in luck, I'd be having something else with my name on it right about now," he drawled wickedly.

Samantha's face went hot as she reached out to offer him a roast beef sandwich, and his eyes feasted on the curve of her breasts, clearly outlined beneath her nylon windbreaker. "Maybe this will tide you over."

Steven took a huge bite, swallowed, then shook his head. "Not for long, Samantha. I'm a very hungry man."

A half hour later, Steven stretched out on his back on the blanket and stared up at the clear blue sky. His stomach was full, but his appetite in another area had yet to be appeased, and the way the day was going, it didn't look like it would be. He loved those kids, but—

No, there weren't any buts about it. He loved them and that was that. Those three high-energy imps made it difficult for him to get their mother alone, but other than that, he had no complaints about them. They were great kids, and Samantha should be commended for the fine job she'd done in raising them. And she'd done it alone.

Samantha refused to talk about her ex-husband, but from all other reports Steven had gathered on the man, Bradley Charles was a blond, blue-eyed charmer who'd believed that his Saturday night drinking habits would be overlooked by the daughter of a full-time drunk. However, shortly after his marriage, his nights out with the boys had lengthened to include the entire weekend, which left him in no shape to work at the lumber mill on Monday mornings. Within a year he'd lost several other jobs and had taken up carousing as a full-time occupation.

"What a scowl," Samantha observed as she sat down next to Steven on the blanket. Keeping one eye on the children, who were off searching for flat rocks they could skip across the deep water of the pool, she began reloading the picnic basket with the remnants of their lunch. "I guess you didn't realize what this outing would be like with three children along. My kids don't know the meaning of the word solitude."

Steven heard the brittle edge to her voice and was quick to reassure her. Maybe this fishing expedition had turned out to be far more hectic than he'd imagined, but it wouldn't help his cause any if she felt he hadn't enjoyed it. "With the exception of one wayward fish hook, I knew exactly what it would be like. I've had plenty of solitude lately, and believe me, it's not all it's cracked up to be."

Samantha's smile was relieved. "But you used to come up here when you wanted to enjoy some peace and quiet."

Steven nodded as he sat up. "That was right after my father died. Suddenly I had all of this responsibility thrust into my lap, and it got pretty overwhelming at times. Armstrong Enterprises employs over five hundred people in six states, and every decision I make affects them, as well as me. Sometimes I just had to get away by myself to think and work everything out in my head to make sure I wasn't making the wrong decisions."

"Well, your head must have worked things out beautifully," Samantha complimented. "The way I hear it, Armstrong Enterprises is even more profitable now than it was when your father was in charge."

Steven shrugged. "I guess."

"You guess?" Samantha exclaimed. "How could there be any doubt in your mind?"

"Oh, I know I'm making more money than my dad ever did, but he made more than enough to support his family. With Rob gone and Conlan married, I don't have any family around anymore. Sometimes I have to ask myself what the hell it is I'm working so hard to create and who's going to appreciate it once I'm gone."

To his surprise and delight, Steven saw that Samantha understood what he was saying and actually sympathized. "You're not going to start playing an invisible violin or make up lyrics about the poor little rich boy, are you?"

Samantha shook her head. In the past week she'd learned quite a bit about Armstrong Enterprises and the demands made upon its chairman of the board. Considering the amount of time and effort Steven spent running his business, Samantha could see why he would question his motives for making more and more profit. After all, how much money did one person require? Steven was a man who had everything but those things that counted most. In one way, at least, she was wealthier than he.

"No," she said evenly. "I understand how you feel. A person needs something to work for besides money. Everything I do is for my children, for their future security and happiness. I love them so much, and I don't think my life would have much meaning without them."

"I want my life to have meaning, too, Samantha," Steven said, and he took a deep breath for courage. With the children off playing, this might be his only chance to declare himself. "When I think about my future, I don't picture myself very happy unless I make some changes in my life. This week I've discovered that I really like having someone to come home to. It's high time I got married. I've gone over my prospects, and only one fabulous lady comes to mind. What do you think of my chances that she'll say yes?"

As the wrenching shock of his question ripped through her, Samantha groped for a normal tone. "What woman would turn down a proposal from the most eligible bachelor in Montana?"

As soon as she said it, she turned her face the other way so Steven wouldn't see the pain she felt picturing him married to some "fabulous lady." If she had known that a mistress was expected to discuss her lover's future marriage prospects, she would've taken an ax to that four-poster bed before she'd ever climbed into it.

"You might," Steven suggested carefully.

Samantha tried to make her laugh sound amused, but she didn't know how successful she was. "But then I'm not a *lady*, so what I might say doesn't matter."

"Dammit, Samantha! There you go putting yourself down again," Steven growled and grabbed hold of her shoulder to turn her around.

"I wasn't putting myself down. I'm accepting reality," Samantha retorted defensively. "I know what I am and what you think of me."

"I happen to think you're wonderful, but it's what you think of me that's at issue here," Steven snapped. "For God's sake, I spent most of last night making love to you, and you have the nerve to suggest I'd get up the next morning and ask somebody else to marry me? What kind of louse do you think I am?"

"I don't think you're a—you were asking *me*?" Samantha squeaked as comprehension hit her.

Steven gazed heavenward as if hoping for divine guidance. "God! I want to marry a woman who's determined to drive me insane! Either that, or she's got a hearing problem."

Samantha stared at him as if she *did* indeed think he'd gone mad. "You're proposing? This is a proposal of marriage?"

"That was my original intent," Steven agreed, his dark eyes still sparking with temper. "Even if my intended doesn't choose to believe it."

"But you hardly know me," Samantha breathed incredulously, her disbelief clearly evident on her face. "Why on earth would you want to marry me when you could have any number of fantastically beautiful, sophisticated women who don't come as a package deal?"

Steven had tried to be romantic, but gave up on the idea that romance was going to have any part in this scenario. When he'd imagined himself proposing to the woman he loved, this wasn't how it was supposed to go, but then, Samantha wasn't the sentimental hearts-and-flowers type. No, his woman was a mistrustful realist who didn't expect anything good to come her way, and even when it did, she had a hard time accepting it.

The only way to convince her that he was sincere was to speak entirely in practicalities. "I don't have time to go out looking for some fantastically beautiful woman, besides which, I find you plenty beautiful enough," Steven complimented. "It's also been my experience, that lovely sophisticates can be pretty useless. I've dated several, and none of them would be happy living in the back of beyond, with nothing to do and no place to use their charge cards."

Satisfied that he'd gotten her full attention and that she was seriously considering what he said, Steven continued, "You, on the other hand, don't seem to mind the isolation, and you know how to make yourself useful. You wouldn't be harping at me all the time to keep you entertained."

From the intent way she was staring at him, Steven could tell he was making progress. "As I said earlier, I want a wife and a family, and if I marry you, I'll have one ready-made. I won't have to wait around to have kids."

If Samantha had any doubts about Steven loving her, they'd just been confirmed. He didn't. He wasn't looking for a woman to love; he wanted one who would cook his meals and clean his house and not make any unreasonable demands on his time. He was a busy man, and to conserve on this precious commodity, he preferred a woman with kids so he wouldn't have to devote himself to the long, tedious business of siring his own.

"I see," Samantha said, looking as if she were actually giving his unromantic proposition some real thought, when in truth, she was fighting back tears of disappointment and outrage. She'd placed Steven up on a pedestal, thinking he was so different from other men, so much better than Brad, but the pedestal was developing some major cracks.

"And you have to admit we're highly compatible in bed. The physical side of our marriage will be great," Steven was saying, and the cracks widened considerably. "Think about it, Samantha. There would be benefits in this arrangement for both of us. I'll be the very best father I can be to your kids, and you'll never have another day's worry over your finances. You know what I'm worth. I can provide all the security you'll ever need."

"There is that," Samantha muttered under her breath, but Steven was too involved in what he was saying to pick up on her sarcastic tone.

"If you want, I can have it all put down in writing before we're married, so you won't have to worry that I'll up and leave you with nothing like your last husband. I'm sure we can work out a satisfactory prenuptial agreement."

*This is getting worse all the time,* Samantha thought, trying hard not to fall apart. Now the lawyer in him wanted to negotiate a contract to make sure there wouldn't be legal trouble from her if their relationship didn't work out, which it wouldn't if he was already planning for the end. "I don't think that will be necessary," she managed to croak out.

"I don't, either," Steven said with a pleased smile. "You know you can trust me."

Samantha smiled back. *Just about as far as I can throw you.*

"So what do you say, Samantha?" Steven asked, unable to think of anything else to add that might aid his cause. "Will you marry me?"

"No."

"No," Steven repeated dumbly. When her refusal finally got through to him, he got angry. "No! What do you mean, no?"

"I thought that answer was fairly clear," Samantha retorted. "No means no, I don't want to marry you."

Steven jumped to his feet and pulled Samantha up by the wrist so they stood toe-to-toe. "Why in hell not?" he demanded in outrage.

"What you say all sounds very nice, but I've heard the same promises before. I'm sorry, Steven, but I've already been married once, and I didn't like it," Samantha raged back.

"That's because you married an irresponsible jerk, but I plan to take care of you for the rest of your life!"

"I don't want to be taken care of," Samantha exclaimed. "I can take care of myself and my children without you or your money. In another year or two, our ranch will start earning enough profit to keep us quite comfortably."

Never before in his life had Steven lost his temper so completely that he didn't think before he spoke.

"What ranch?" he demanded. "You don't own a ranch—I own it, and I'll be damned before I'll let you go back there!"

All the color drained out of Samantha's face. "You're lying! I possess a copy of the deed."

Steven reached out and grasped her by the shoulders, forcing her to hear him out. "What you have is nothing but a worthless copy. I've got the original with Caleb's signature turning the property over to me. He sold it, Samantha! He sold it to me the year before he died."

"No," Samantha denied. "Please tell me it isn't true." But she could see that it was, she could read the truth in Steven's eyes.

Steven watched her face as the information sank in and cursed himself a hundred times over. "I'm sorry," he apologized, raking one hand through his hair. "Sooner or later, I had to tell you, but I didn't mean for you to find out this way. I never thought…oh hell, I was conceited enough to think you'd jump at the chance to marry me. I planned on breaking this to you after you'd agreed to become my wife. I figured it wouldn't have mattered to you so much then."

Samantha lifted her chin in the way that was becoming very familiar to Steven. He could see now that it *did* matter. It mattered terribly, but she was determined not to let it show.

With all the dignity at her command, she admitted, "Well, it appears now that I need a husband twice as badly as you need a wife. Is your offer to marry me still open?"

Steven didn't move and couldn't breathe. This wasn't right, not right at all. He didn't want her marrying him because she felt she had no other choice, but that's what he'd accomplished with his short temper and big mouth. It was just that, after last night he'd assumed that she felt more for him than desire, and when he'd found out that she didn't, it had hurt—badly enough that he'd lashed out at her without thinking.

"I won't bulldoze you into doing something you don't want to do," he said, barely able to hold her gaze without being overcome by the despair in her eyes.

Samantha lifted her chin another notch. "I'll marry you, Steven. I already know you're a wonderful lover, and you've promised to be a good father and generous provider. What more could I want in a husband?"

# Nine

**A** few hours after the marriage ceremony, the resigned-looking groom, followed closely on the heels by his best man, stepped into his study and closed the door. Tall, powerfully built men, they were both dressed in white shirts and dark suits, and almost simultaneously they shrugged out of their jackets and loosened their collars. As they reached for the knots on their ties, they took note of their mutual actions and exchanged commensurate grins.

"Too much starch," they said at the same time, and they laughed at the inside joke dating back to their adolescence.

"I'm glad you could come on such short notice," Steven said, once their amusement had passed.

"I wouldn't have missed this event for all the tea in China," Conlan Fox drawled meaningfully.

Steven glanced up for a moment, then quickly back down again, shuffling a few papers around on his desk so he wouldn't have to meet Conlan's all-too-knowing gaze. Not for the first time today, Steven regretted that there hadn't been enough time for Robert to make it out for the wedding. His easygoing younger brother would have kept the jokes and laughter coming so fast that Conlan wouldn't have noticed a certain lack of bliss between the bride and groom.

Steven dared another glance at his best friend only to find Conlan's discerning blue eyes centered squarely on his face. "I...um...hope the ride down from your place on that bumpy track you call a road wasn't too hard on Kerry," he spoke again swiftly, dropping into the chair behind his desk and reaching for a decanter of brandy. "It was nice for Samantha to have a woman stand up with her today, but neither of us expected Kerry to come when she's this far into her pregnancy, especially her first."

Conlan Fox took the leather chair facing the desk, trying not to smile as he listened to Steven ramble on. He'd spent too many years living under the same roof with this man not to recognize his evasive tactics. Even as a kid, Steven had been an expert at directing conversation away from subjects he didn't wish to discuss, but this time Conlan wasn't going to let him get away with it. A little over a year ago, Steven had taken an unholy pleasure in interrogating him about his love life. This time, Conlan decided, it was his turn to ask the questions.

"Kerry's over eight months along. If the baby came a little early, it would be fine. Anyway, everyone tells me first babies tend to come late," Conlan said in a deceptively placid tone as he leaned back in the chair and stretched his long legs out before him. He watched Steven carefully as he poured them each a brandy, noting the visible tremor in his hand. Even on his wedding day, the Steven he knew wouldn't have been half as nervous as he had been today.

"So, when is yours due?" Conlan inquired abruptly as soon as Steven had taken the first swallow of his own drink.

Once Steven had recovered from his spat of coughing, he choked out irately, "Samantha's not pregnant!"

"Well, you can't blame me for wondering," Conlan said. "Considering that I talked to you only a couple of weeks ago and you never mentioned the woman, it sure seemed to me like this was some sort of shotgun wedding. All during the ceremony I had no reason to think otherwise since the bride looked about ready to faint, and the groom looked like he was facing the firing squad instead of a preacher."

Steven took another big swallow of brandy. "So, I was nervous," he muttered defensively. "And if I recall, you weren't all smiles the day you walked down the aisle."

That accusation inspired a hearty chuckle. "I can still remember how hard my knees were knocking," Conlan admitted. "I've never been so scared in my life."

"After leading the bachelor life for so long, marriage is a big step," Steven agreed, thinking he'd talked his way around Conlan's concerns.

He'd thought wrong. Conlan wasn't about to let him off the hook so easily. "At least my wife didn't look horrified at the mention of a honeymoon."

Steven's dismissing shrug was less than convincing. "Samantha was surprised by the arrangements, that's all. I shouldn't have sprung it on her like that."

Conlan appeared to accept that explanation. "And I suppose she could feel a bit uneasy about leaving her children with someone they don't know. Aunt Polly is great with kids, but three days without mom can seem an awfully long time to a four-year-old."

Steven elaborated on that possibility. "Heather's very attached to her mother, and I'm certain Samantha's never left her or the boys with anyone before. As far as I know, they don't have any close relatives."

Conlan might have stopped baiting him if Steven hadn't clamped on to that pitiful excuse like a hungry trout, but since he had, Conlan decided to set the hook and reel him in. "If you ask me, those kids are a lot less worried about being left alone with Aunt Polly than their mother is at being left alone with you."

Steven swallowed the bait—hook, line and sinker. "So, who asked you!"

Without saying a word, Conlan folded his arms over his chest and waited patiently for Steven to tangle himself even further. He didn't have to wait long. "Dammit, Con! Just because Samantha and I aren't— hell! Where do you get off prying into my personal business?"

"Now, that question has a familiar ring to it," Conlan observed dryly. "Only the last time I heard it, it was coming from me."

"That was different!" Steven insisted. "If someone hadn't interfered, you and Kerry would never have gotten together. Samantha and I may have our problems, but we're already married, so you can just butt out!"

Conlan cocked his head to one side, obviously thinking back to that earlier conversation when Steven had forced him to admit that he was as hopelessly in love as Steven appeared to be. "Hmm... what was it you said when I asked you to butt out? Oh, yes, now I remember. *I'm your best friend, and I'm only trying to do you a favor.*"

At Steven's sour look, Conlan changed his tone and became serious. "We're like brothers, Steven, and I care about you. I've always been able to tell when something's seriously bothering you. I know you're used to handling everything yourself. I am, too, but I've learned that it sometimes helps if you can talk to somebody else about it, someone who's been there."

"Been where?"

"Been so much in love that he aches all over and so terrified that the woman he loves doesn't feel the same way. Last year you helped me own up to my feelings about Kerry, now it's my turn to help you."

This was the first time in Steven's recollection that Conlan had been so forthcoming about his emotions. Part Absaroka Indian, Conlan had always seemed so self-contained, but the love of a beautiful woman had brought about some miraculous changes. Steven couldn't help but envy him, knowing that he wasn't going to reap the same kind of benefits from his marriage. "I know I love Samantha—my problem is that

Samantha doesn't love me, and I doubt she ever will. I blackmailed her into marrying me."

Not much could shock Conlan, but Steven's surprise confession did. "You what?"

The incredulous look on Conlan's face made Steven grit his teeth. "I find it hard to believe, myself, but that's what I did."

"Why would you resort to something so underhanded?" Conlan wanted to know. "Good Lord, Steven, you've always been able to get any woman you wanted."

Steven's laugh was self-deprecating. "Not this one."

After that equally astonishing admission, the entire story came out. By the time he'd heard it all, Conlan was shaking his head in commiseration. "It's not your fault that her father sold out to you."

"Try telling Samantha that," Steven suggested grimly. "As far as she's concerned, I'm the ruthless lord of the manor, and in order to get what I want, I stepped all over her dreams. Ever since I met her, I've done nothing but make mistakes."

"Now I *know* this is the real thing," Conlan said, smiling sympathetically. "The minute I clapped eyes on Kerry, I couldn't seem to do a damned thing right."

Steven wished he was in the position to smile back, but he wasn't. "Tell me about it. You should've heard my marriage proposal. Instead of pledging my undying love, I thought I'd stand a better chance of her saying yes if I appealed to her sense of practicality. I made it sound like I was willing to pay her very generously in return for warming my bed and cooking and keeping house. I even offered to draw up a prenuptial contract and make the bargain legal!''

Conlan winced. "Oh, brother, do you ever have your work cut out for you."

Steven threw up his hands. "What the hell can I do about it now? It's too late for a retraction. I've tried talking to her, but she won't listen. She doesn't believe a word I say."

Conlan stood up from the chair and placed his empty glass down on the desk. "Then don't use words," Conlan advised. "Take her up to the lodge and make love to her so many times and in so many ways that she can't help but believe you."

That advice did inspire a brief chuckle. "Is that why it took so long for you and Kerry to come down from your mountain and announce your engagement?"

Conlan's blue eyes sparkled wickedly. "Take my word for it, pal. When you can't find the right words, it's time for some action."

Steven took a deep breath and nodded in agreement. "Okay, but if you never hear from us again, just remember that it was your bright idea."

Up on the second floor, Kerry Fox was dispensing an equal share of unsolicited advice and unqualified support to Samantha. Unlike the trouble Conlan had getting Steven to talk, Kerry had no such difficulty with Steven's new wife. The poor thing had entered the bedroom to change out of her wedding clothes and promptly burst into tears before she'd undone the first button at the back of her pale blue dress.

The whole story had come out between sobs, but even after she'd heard it, Kerry couldn't believe it.

"You're wrong, Samantha," she insisted. "I know Steven. He's a kind, wonderful man. He'd never marry a woman he didn't love just to have a convenient bed partner and a full-time housekeeper. All he'd have to do is snap his fingers, and a dozen volunteers would come running."

"That many!" Samantha exclaimed, and if anything, looked even more miserable than she had during the wedding ceremony. Covering her pale face in both hands, she gave in to the weakness in her legs and sat down on the bed. "There's no way I can compete with all those other women he knows."

"Horsepucky," Kerry declared resolutely, proud of herself for coming up with a word that she couldn't have conceived of herself saying a year ago. "You love him, don't you?"

"Yes," Samantha replied softly, but a wealth of unhappiness could be heard in that one small word.

"Well, then, everything else will work itself out." As her sympathetic gaze fell on Steven's tearful bride, Kerry was struck by the irony of this situation. The biggest problem she'd had in dealing with Conlan was throwing off the cloak of gentility she'd worn since childhood, while Samantha's problem with Steven was never having owned one.

"You probably don't know this about me, Samantha," Kerry said in an attempt to reassure the woman. "But I've got more wealth and breeding than I know what to do with. Like Steven, I'm one of those filthy rich Armstrongs, and I've always had everything you think you lack."

Samantha lowered her hands and stared up at Kerry in astonishment. They'd only known each other a few hours, but from the first minute, Samantha had felt a real kinship with the other woman. Kerry was as small as she was, with a wild tangle of red hair, and dimples that practically beamed good cheer. Married a little over a year, she and Conlan were starting a ranch in the Absaroka Mountains, even though Kerry didn't seem any more fit for the job than Samantha had been.

For some reason, when Steven had told her that Conlan and Kerry lived in a small rustic cabin and had just gotten hot- and cold-running water, she'd assumed that the couple wasn't very well off, an assumption that had made her feel as if she and Kerry had so much in common. Now Kerry was telling her that she was everything Samantha wanted to be, but wasn't.

"But do you know something?" Kerry asked, easing her petite, very pregnant body onto a chair. "When I met Conlan, all that tasteful old money and refined good breeding became the source of my biggest problems. Conlan refused to touch a dime of my fortune, and he couldn't believe I was strong enough to share his kind of life. You wouldn't believe the kind of extremes I had to go to in order to convince him otherwise."

Leaning back on the soft cushions, she rolled her eyes. "Men can be so blind at times, and from what you've just told me, they aren't the only ones. What would you rather have, Samantha? Your precious independence or the man you love? Though it's beyond me why you think you can't be an independent woman and a loving wife at the same time."

"Because I have next to nothing to contribute to this relationship," Samantha cried. "It's completely one-sided. Steven gives me everything, and in return I clean his house and make sure he gets three square meals a day."

"You can contribute the only thing that matters in any relationship," Kerry stated quietly. "You can love that man as he deserves to be loved. That's something no amount of money can buy, and Steven must know it, or he wouldn't have married you."

*But money can buy other things.* Samantha's gaze traveled to the suitcase lying open on the bed. Steven had not only arranged for a honeymoon without consulting her, but he'd also gone out and purchased the appropriate wardrobe. Every sexy frill and lovely bit of French lace reminded her of what Steven expected to get out of their marriage besides domestic help, and it sure as heck wasn't love.

"I can love him from now till doomsday," Samantha exclaimed. "But that doesn't mean he's ever going to love me back. He desires me, yes, but how long can that last?"

"From the way Steven looks at you," Kerry replied, "I'd say you don't have a thing to worry about until doomsday comes."

Samantha's eyes widened with a glimmer of hope. "You really think so?"

"Without a doubt." Kerry's smile was huge as she patted her gigantic stomach. "I can see how much Steven adores your children, but I hope you're prepared to go through this again. With all the comments he made about liking the sound of running feet, I have the feeling Steven is planning to add a few more.''

A dreamy expression came into Samantha's eyes as she thought about being pregnant with Steven's baby, but she sobered quickly when she noticed Kerry's knowing smile and twinkling green eyes. ''I won't be having any more children,'' she vowed stiffly. ''Since I know that without love this marriage can't last, it wouldn't be fair to them.''

''But you wish it would last, don't you?'' Kerry inquired.

Samantha nodded. ''But that would be like wishing for the moon.''

''I'm not too sure of that,'' Kerry stated firmly. ''As I told you before, Samantha, I know Steven, and he's very much like Con. They're both so strong willed and forceful, it's easy to assume that they wouldn't need anyone, but nothing could be farther from the truth.''

Samantha thought about the loneliness she sometimes glimpsed in Steven's eyes, and she knew that Kerry was right. ''Steven *does* need someone. I'm just not sure that someone is me.''

''But Steven is,'' Kerry said. ''If he wasn't, you wouldn't be wearing that ring.''

Samantha looked down at the shiny gold band on her finger. ''He wouldn't have had to marry me,'' she murmured as if that fact had just dawned on her.

Kerry laughed. ''But he did, and since he has, I doubt very much that he'll ever allow you to leave him. Take my word for it, men like Steven and Con have a tendency to be very possessive when it comes to their wives and children. I know being thought of as some man's possession goes against the feminist grain, but I predict that Steven will make it up to you in other ways. Con can be so sweet, at times it makes me want to cry."

"I know the feeling," Samantha whispered in despair. Steven sometimes said or did things that made her heart swell to the point of bursting; kind, wonderful things that made her love him all the more. Yet as much as she adored him, she also feared that their marriage was doomed. What she felt for Steven was love, but it was highly possible that he'd gotten that emotion mixed up with the blazing desire they set off in one another.

From painful experience, Samantha knew that passion flamed hot, but burned out just as quickly. With a wistful sigh, Samantha murmured, "If only marriage came with a lifetime guarantee for success."

Kerry shook her head, hiding her smile behind a silky curtain of red hair. Samantha didn't know it yet, and Kerry couldn't say anything to convince her, but a written guarantee wouldn't be necessary. Being an Armstrong herself, Kerry was fully confident that eventually this marriage was going to work out just fine. Steven was much too stubborn a man to allow any other outcome.

"If you want my advice," Kerry said, "I'd take advantage of these three days to sit down and have a long, serious talk with your husband, get all your feelings out in the open."

"I don't know what good talking's going to do."

"I haven't been married that long," Kerry admitted. "But one thing I've learned is that good verbal communication is the key to every problem. Let Steven know how you're feeling."

"How I feel doesn't matter."

Kerry gave an exasperated sigh. "I don't know how you came by your inferiority complex, Samantha, but it's high time you got rid of it. You're a mature, capable woman who's responsible for three kids, and you deserve to know where you stand in this marriage."

Knowing Samantha still lacked the kind of confidence she herself had, Kerry went on. "Maybe you'll find out that Steven doesn't love you, but that doesn't mean he won't come to love you later on, or that you've entered into a bad marriage. If you respect each other and are both willing to make an honest commitment, everything should work out fine. After all, compatibility is a prime necessity for a strong, lasting relationship."

"And great sex is the only basis for our compatibility," Samantha muttered sadly.

"I think you're selling Steven awfully short," Kerry admonished. "Give the poor man a chance, Samantha. He didn't have to marry you to get a great sexual partner, but if you still believe that, don't hop into bed with him until you've talked everything out. I'm betting you'll be very pleasantly surprised with the results."

"Maybe," Samantha said, but as she stared down at her wedding band, she felt a new sense of resolve.

For better or worse, she was married, so what did she have to lose by trying?

With a determined lift of her chin, she declared, "Okay, Kerry. I'll accept that bet, but I hope you're prepared to pay up when we get back."

Kerry laughed. "I'm not the least bit worried. Believe me, Samantha, sex may be the most important aspect of an affair, but good verbal communication is the mainstay of any successful marriage."

*Talk. We're not doing anything until we talk.*

Samantha sat staring out the window of Steven's black Mercedes, which she hadn't even known he owned, experiencing a sensation that hovered somewhere between anxiety and panic. Her stomach was tied up in knots, and with every mile that drew them higher into the mountains, the knots tightened. The Armstrong hunting lodge was only twenty miles away, less than a half hour drive, and Steven didn't look as if he was in the mood to do much talking once they got there. In fact, according to the anticipatory gleam in his eyes, he had something else in mind entirely.

"Your Aunt Polly is quite a character," Samantha said in an attempt to get some sort of conversation going. "Is she always like that?"

"Uh-huh," Steven replied absently, his mind clearly on other matters. Then, as if he thought her question was inspired by undue concern, he glanced over at her. "You're not worried about leaving the kids with her, are you?"

Samantha couldn't help but smile at that idea. Within minutes of her introduction, Polly Mc-

Pherson had had both Zack and Heather eating out of her hand, and Tony had capitulated as soon as she'd mentioned her belief that chocolate cake was a suitable bedtime snack. With her snowy-white hair, generous mouth and rosy cheeks, the elderly woman came across as a tall, robust version of Mrs. Santa.

"I'm not worried at all," Samantha said. "It's obvious that she loves children and knows exactly how to handle them. It was very kind of her to drop everything and come stay with them so we could have a honeymoon."

"She doesn't mind. Taking care of little kids is Polly's speciality," Steven informed her. "The whole year-round she travels from one family to the next until she's seen all fourteen of her nieces and nephews. Now that I've got my own children, we'll be added to the list of her annual stops."

*Now that I've got my own children.* Samantha's heart warmed at Steven's choice of words. No matter how he viewed their mother, he truly had accepted her kids as his own. Maybe Kerry was right. Maybe their marriage *did* stand a chance.

It wasn't Steven's fault if he didn't know where she was coming from half the time. Once she'd opened up to him, told him why it had seemed so important to own her own place, maybe he would comprehend her reasons for being so frightened about commiting herself to another man. All of her life, she'd lived under the influence of men under the influence, and it had warped her perspective on males and on life in general.

As the child of Caleb Todd, she'd been labeled trash at an early age, and now she knew that most people thought she'd lived up to that label when she'd married Brad Charles. Foolishly she'd believed Brad when he'd vowed to love, honor and cherish her until death do us part, but she, above anyone else, should have known that the promises of an alcoholic were worthless. In the end she'd been forced to live with the knowledge that she'd escaped a lousy home life only to marry the same kind of man as her father. To make matters worse, she'd had three kids before she'd finally accepted the truth.

Making a go of the ranch had been her way of improving her damaged self-confidence, of learning to trust in her own judgment again. It had also seemed like an opportunity to change the poor expectations placed on her by others. She'd needed to prove her own worth, to herself and to her children. That's why she'd been so devastated when she'd found out that Steven owned her land.

Without that ranch, she no longer had the means to convince anyone that she could succeed on her own. Steven had the ability to provide everything any woman could want, but the more generous he became, the more worthless she felt. She hoped that once she explained this to Steven, he would try to understand that need to feel as if she were giving as much as she was taking in this relationship. She would always be grateful to Kerry Fox for showing her just how she might accomplish that goal.

Kerry had been right in saying that it was time she got rid of her inferiority complex. She did have something to offer Steven—something priceless. In exchange for all the material wealth and security Steven would provide her with, she could love him as he deserved to be loved. Although she was frightened by the risk she was about to take, Samantha was prepared to give Steven all the love she had to give.

On the other side of the front seat, Steven was fighting to control his own anxieties. *Make love to her so many times and in so many ways that she can't help but believe you.*

Intellectually speaking, Steven could fully embrace the logic behind Conlan's advice, but a doubting inner voice kept asking questions, like what was he going to do if it didn't work? Or how would he ever handle it if Samantha resented him and the circumstances that had brought about their marriage for the rest of their married life?

Unable to think about that possibility without experiencing a feeling of sick dread, Steven arrived at a decision. It didn't make him entirely comfortable, but it was the best plan he could devise under present circumstances. No matter what happened, he wasn't going to let Samantha out of his bed until she was absolutely certain that he loved her with all the power of his being.

Realizing that they were less than ten minutes away from their destination, Steven hurriedly broke the silence. If he was going to act on Conlan's advice, he'd better start laying down some groundwork. "You looked absolutely beautiful today," he said. "That blue dress matched your gorgeous eyes."

"Thank you," Samantha replied with a gasp at the unexpected compliment. Beauty was definitely in the eye of the beholder, for as far as she was concerned, she'd never looked worse in her life than she had this morning.

"And now that we're married, you look even more beautiful to me," Steven continued, encouraged by her delighted flush. He racked his brain for other suitable compliments, but ended up with a trite observation about her clothes. "If possible, you look even better in pink. That sweater you're wearing brings out the color in your cheeks and adds a lovely glow to your hair."

Samantha glanced down dubiously at her pink angora sweater and matching wool pants, which were over five years old. "I'm glad you think so," she said, anxious to meet him halfway, since she'd acted so distant and cold to him in the days before their marriage. Unfortunately she was so nervous that all she could think of to say was that he looked very handsome.

Steven beamed at her, his brown eyes darkening with pleasure as if she'd just flattered him with a line of classic romantic poetry. "We're going to be happy together, Samantha," he vowed. "You'll see."

Somehow their insipid exchange of compliments had confirmed something in Steven's mind, but Samantha didn't quite share his confidence. "Maybe," she allowed. "But we've got a lot of talking to do first. There are so many things I need to say to you."

Steven could well imagine what Samantha wished to say, and he didn't want to hear it. "If we try, I'm sure we can work out all our problems," he insisted. Silently he added, *And we're going to start working as soon as we get to the lodge.*

# Ten

Like a gallant knight of old, Steven lifted Samantha out of the car and carried her across the muddy ruts in the graveled drive. She barely had enough time to register that the Armstrong hunting lodge looked more like a Swiss chalet, before she was lifted over the threshold and swept inside.

"Welcome to my private lair, Mrs. Armstrong, where at last I can do what I've been wanting to do all day," Steven said with a wolfish smile before covering her mouth with his in an all-consuming kiss.

Samantha stopped thinking the instant his tongue delved into her mouth. Steven's kisses always commanded her full attention, and heaven help her, this time was no different than any other. For all her good intentions to talk first and make love later, she couldn't find the strength to pull her lips away from the tempting ardor of his.

Samantha was completely breathless by the time Steven lowered her to her feet, and while she struggled to regain her bearings, he pulled her along with him into the great room. He came to a stop in the center of the room, let go of her hand and waited to hear her reaction. "This doesn't look like any hunting lodge I've ever seen," she managed when she eventually found her voice again.

Steven chuckled, enjoying her obvious astonishment. "Romantic, isn't it?" he inquired in a husky tone. "The perfect place for our honeymoon."

Samantha didn't dare meet his gaze, knowing his eyes were glowing with the sensual promise of what was to come. "It ... um ... it's very nice."

Steven grinned at her, very much aware that she was still off balance from his devastating kisses. Now all he had to do was keep her that way until he was able to prove to her that she hadn't made a mistake by marrying him. "This was Mom and Dad's getaway place," he informed her. "They always told us kids they were taking off to do some hunting, but I doubt that was the purpose they had in mind when they came up here."

Samantha doubted it, too. Instead of the sturdy, masculine furniture, rustic hardwood floors and massive stone fireplace she'd been expecting, this cozy haven was carpeted in a plush oyster-blue pile. The country French furniture was upholstered in a soft floral design and the freestanding fireplace was made of white enamel, enclosed on three sides with glass.

In place of the hunting trophies she expected to see mounted on dark wood paneling, the light, cream-colored walls were decorated with lovely oil paintings, framed cross-stitch samplers and curio shelves displaying treasured family mementos. The only concession to the ridiculous notion that this was a hunting lodge was the soft white fur rug spread out before the fireplace and a matching white pelt draped over the back of a cushy chaise lounge.

At the far corner of the room, beneath a delicate crystal chandelier, was a small round table and two upholstered chairs. Next to the table was a rich, hand-hewn buffet with an interior light that showed off a collection of pewter dinnerware. Steven opened an antique cabinet with a flourish, exposing a television, VCR and stereo.

First dinner, then dancing, then seduction, Samantha thought uneasily as she glanced over at Steven and caught him smiling to himself. There was no doubt in her mind that this was the plan he intended to put into action as quickly as possible. They hadn't made love since that first time, and she was very much aware that Steven was fast losing his patience. From his point of view, there was no longer any reason for them to wait.

As her eyes traveled up the circular staircase leading to the sleeping loft, Samantha felt a growing sense of doom. Looking under the polished oak railing, she could see a huge old-fashioned brass bed. Right down to the thick feather mattress, this place was the perfect love nest, a private refuge, completely cut off from the rest of the world. Slanted windows let in the last dying rays of the sun and also provided a panoramic view of the snowcapped mountains.

"How do you like it so far?" Steven inquired as Samantha turned away from the stairs and walked toward a swinging door which she supposed led to the kitchen.

"How could anyone not like it?" Samantha replied as she pushed open the door and walked through to explore the quaint kitchen. Gleaming copper pots hung over the black cast-iron stove, and a large copper bowl sat in the middle of the short trestle table. The room seemed old-fashioned, yet all the modern conveniences were available, including a built-in dishwasher.

Samantha was so enchanted by her surroundings that she didn't notice when Steven joined her, and she jumped at the sound of his voice. "Ta...da," he exclaimed dramatically as he pulled open the door of the refrigerator. "I sent Chuck up here yesterday to make sure we had enough food.

"Hmm. What have we here?" Reaching inside, he drew out a chilled bottle of champagne and two crystal goblets. "Well, what do you know about that?" he declared in surprise. "It's not only French, but a great year. Chuck has more class than I thought."

A week ago, even a day ago, Samantha would have reacted poorly to the realization that when it came to champagne, she wouldn't know a good year from a bad one. However, instead of feeling inferior, she found herself appreciating the shy foreman's sweet gesture. Stepping forward, she pointed at one of the goblets. "Look, he's even had our names etched into the glass."

"Who would've guessed that beneath that stoic exterior beats a sentimental heart?" Steven asked as he set the bottle down on the counter. "To show our appreciation, we'll have to offer him the first toast."

Samantha could hardly refuse to drink when a few moments later Steven handed her a glass of champagne and put action to words. "To Chuck," he said simply as he clinked his goblet against hers and lifted it to his mouth.

As his warm gaze met hers, Samantha's mouth went so dry that she finished off every drop of champagne in her glass. Steven immediately filled it again and offered a second toast. "To us."

"To us," Samantha repeated, and again she foolishly drained the glass to the very last drop, forgetting what kind of impact alcohol had on a person who rarely drank and one who'd had nothing to eat since noon. Within seconds the knots in her stomach began to loosen, and a pleasant warmth eased the constrictions in her chest. Feeling much more relaxed, she wasn't averse to Steven's suggestion that they take their champagne to the table in the great room so they could enjoy the prepared tray of cold cuts and cheese he removed from the refrigerator.

"All of a sudden, I'm starving," Samantha admitted as she preceded him out of the kitchen, stumbling slightly as her feet passed from the tiled floor to the thick pile carpeting.

"Me, too," Steven agreed, but if Samantha had turned around she would've been aware that his mind wasn't on food. His eyes lingered much too long on the curve of her spine, blatantly caressed the slender outline of her hips and joyfully studied the delightful motion of her derriere as she walked.

*So far so good,* Steven thought to himself as they sat down, and he noted the rosy flush in her cheeks. The champagne was already starting to do its job, and Samantha was beginning to relax. A little more time, a bit more to drink, and she would be putty in his hands.

"Steven," Samantha began as soon as he sat down in the chair opposite hers. "I think there should be total honesty between us and so I—"

"The luggage!" Steven clapped himself on the head and shot up from his seat. "I forgot all about it."

Ready to launch into the speech she'd been practicing for what seemed like hours, Samantha frowned at the interruption. "It's still early." With a determined gleam in her eyes, she continued, "And I won't need anything from my suitcase before we finish eating."

Maybe she didn't, but Steven did. "I brought some tapes for the VCR, and they'll be ruined if they get cold." Refilling her glass, he said, "I'll only be a minute."

The minute stretched into ten, then fifteen, and by the time he returned, Samantha had begun to wonder if she'd been deserted. Having nothing better to do while he was gone, she'd eaten several cheese-laden crackers and washed them all down with another half glass of champagne. "I didn't think we came up here to watch movies," she commented somewhat tartly when Steven finally came back through the door.

"There's movies, and then there are movies," he replied in a wicked tone as he set their cases down at the bottom of the stairs.

Samantha's eyes widened. Did he think she was going to need help getting turned on? After the way she'd been treating him for the past several days, she could understand how he might think that, but he couldn't have been more wrong. "Steven," she said with a sigh. "We *really* do have to talk."

Steven thought he'd stayed outside long enough to distract her from that goal, but the ploy hadn't worked any better than filling her up with champagne had. Even tipsy, she was bound and determined to lay all her cards on the table and let him know exactly how she felt about his forcing her into this marriage. If he wanted to prevent her from telling him what a mistake she thought they'd just made, he had to get her into bed and pronto.

The only weapon he had on his side was her physical susceptibility to his advances, and now was the time to advance. Steven walked back to the table, but instead of sitting down in his chair, he drew Samantha up out of hers. "This is what people are supposed to do on their honeymoon," he whispered hoarsely, hoping she didn't hear the note of pleading in his voice as he kissed one corner of her mouth.

"Oh, Steven," Samantha murmured softly, discovering that her legs were so rubbery that in order to remain upright she had to hold on to him.

"Kiss me, Samantha," he urged. "You know you want to."

"Of course I want to, but—"

Unwilling to hear any buts, Steven claimed her mouth. He opened her lips with his and began a searching motion with his tongue that inspired such a delicious explosion of feeling in her that she almost gave in. "You...you're trying to distract me," she accused, but her exasperation dissolved beneath the warmth of his next kiss and the tantalizing feel of his caressing hands moving over her body.

"I like distracting you," Steven admitted without remorse as he lifted her up in his arms. Never breaking the kiss, he strode swiftly toward the stairs. A few moments later, Samantha found herself lying on top of a quilted bedspread, and Steven was coming down on top of her.

"We...need to talk," she reminded him shakily, but her breathless words didn't slow down Steven's progress at all. With purposeful hands he pulled up her sweater, making her jerk with a sudden spasm of pleasure as he blatantly caressed her swelling breasts and taut nipples. "Not yet, Steven," she managed. "You mustn't."

"Oh, yes I must...we must," Steven murmured thickly, and then his head was against her body, taking her nipple inside the warmth of his mouth, teasing it with his tongue. "You need this as badly as I do."

Where Steven was concerned, Samantha didn't know how to hold back, and he'd caught her completely off guard with this overwhelming sensual ambush. Before she was able to form any kind of protest, things had gone too far for her to deny her own passion. She wasn't aware of when it had happened, or how, but suddenly her sweater and bra were completely gone. Seconds later so was everything else, and Steven was slipping his hands eagerly over her nude body, finding and enjoying the sweet curves of hips and thighs.

Helpless in the throes of her rapidly mounting pleasure, Samantha's arms stole around Steven's neck. Within moments she was as eager as he was to taste the excitement that was always there between them, just waiting for release. Words and speeches were forgotten as she discovered that his clothes had mysteriously disappeared along with hers. She could feel the hard, warm muscles of his naked body, his throbbing arousal against the sensitive skin of her inner thighs, and the need to be one with him intensified until it overcame her desire for anything else—everything else.

Steven felt Samantha's reaction to his need and took ruthless advantage of it. He kissed her again and again, fiery kisses, arousing kisses, kisses that left her breathless. His mouth blazed a path down her throat and his hands surrounded her breasts with a rough, yet tender, touch. He teased her nipples, laving them with his tongue, then took full suckle.

"I need you, Samantha," he muttered, lifting his head as her body arched beneath him in wild abandon. "I'll always need you."

Samantha raked her fingers through his hair, assuring him that she was as hungry as he was when he stroked the soft, silken flesh between her thighs. As he sought and found the tiny center of her sensation, she convulsed in a sudden, delicate release. She surged upward, instinctively seeking the fullness of him, and

Steven was absorbed into the vortex of passion that spiraled around them both.

It was a long time before either of them came back completely to reality. Samantha was aware that Steven hadn't left her body. He was still lying on top of her, his weight pushing her into the soft feather mattress. She could feel the sheen of dampness on his skin. He felt heavy and replete, a sexually satisfied male.

But then as her brain slowly cleared, Samantha realized that sexual satisfaction would never be enough for her, and with that realization came frustration, then anger. Was she destined to succumb to his passion whenever he so much as snapped his fingers? Before she could stop herself, she was pounding on his shoulders and wailing, "Dammit, Steven. We were supposed to talk. I told you I wanted to talk!"

Steven was shocked by the fury in her eyes and stupefied by the blows raining down on him. In self-preservation he flattened her small body beneath his massive weight until she ran out of strength to keep up the fight. Then as she lay gasping for air, he sat up beside her and demanded, "What the devil's got into you? You loved every minute of what just happened, and you'll love it the next time, too!"

"Oh, no, I won't," Samantha warned. "I won't be used like that again!"

"Used!" Steven shouted, incensed that their love-making could inspire such an accusation. "That was love, lady! And if you don't believe it now, you will the next time or the time after that or as many times as it takes to convince you."

Outraged by what she saw as a threat, Samantha retorted, "Using sex as a weapon will only convince me that you're a cruel, insensitive jerk who doesn't deserve to be loved the way I love you!"

Shaking an accusing finger under his nose, she raged on, "Kerry advised me to talk to you, but I can see now that her faith in you was misplaced. You don't care how I feel about anything! All you care about is being sexually satisfied."

Steven opened his mouth to lash back at her with a few choice words that were guaranteed to curl her pink little toes, but then his brain stopped reacting to her anger and picked up on what she'd actually said. *She loves me! She just admitted that she loves me!*

That piece of information left him too stunned to deal with it, so he latched on to the second part of her statement. Grabbing hold of her wrist, he pulled Samantha up into a seated position and stared down into her face. "Hold on there. Kerry advised you? Advised you how?"

Samantha tried to pull her arm out of his grasp, but Steven was much too strong, and he refused to let go. Since she couldn't possibly overpower him, she lifted her chin in defiance and smote him with the fiery temper in her eyes. In a scoffing tone, she blazed, "Kerry suggested I give you a chance to prove that our relationship is based on something besides sex. She told me to sit down and have a serious talk with you, to try and resolve our problems verbally instead of under the sheets."

In a smug tone, she quoted the other woman, "Sexual compatibility is important, but good verbal communication is the mainstay of any successful marriage."

To Samantha's horror and disbelief, Steven burst out laughing. Shaking his head, he blurted, "I don't believe this. It's all-fired ridiculous!"

Samantha was so upset by his reaction that she gave him a good swift kick that hurt her bare toes far worse than his hard shin. "The mere thought of discussing anything with me is ridiculous?" she shrieked. "Ridiculous!"

Still laughing, Steven reached out and grabbed her foot and began kissing her injured toes. "Calm down, honey. I'm not laughing at you. I agree that we need to talk, but first let me tell you what advice Conlan gave me."

His loving attention to her feet appeased Samantha enough for her to say, "Conlan gave *you* some advice?"

Steven nodded, unaware that he was now massaging her foot between his warm hands and sending delightful shivers up Samantha's leg. "I told him my problems with you, and he suggested that I keep you in bed and make love to you until you were thoroughly convinced that I love you. 'When you can't find the words, take action,' he said. I was given to understand that such caveman tactics have worked wonders with Kerry."

"But she thinks..." Samantha trailed off as the irony of their situation struck her. "Oh, dear," she said before erupting with laughter. "And we—I—? Well, no wonder you thought what Kerry said to me was so funny, when Conlan told you the complete opposite."

Steven was quick to deny that assumption. "Funny for them maybe, but not us. Those two busybodies almost ruined our day-old marriage."

"No, they didn't," Samantha denied with a laugh, a feeling of effervescent joy bubbling up inside her. "Actually I think we owe them a huge debt of thanks."

"How so?" Steven inquired dubiously.

"For you to follow Conlan's stupid advice you must really love me," she replied simply, her eyes shining with wonder.

"Well, you embraced Kerry's idiotic philosophy every bit as fast," Steven retorted, a similar glow in his own eyes. "So you must love me, too."

"Exactly," Samantha said. "We still have some talking to do, and we probably need to make love several more times, but knowing what we know now, half the battle is already over."

Steven's lips curved upward in a lascivious smile as he accepted her logic. "So it is," he agreed, and he slid his fingers up farther on her leg. "On the advice of our two good friends, first we make love, then we talk."

"We've already made love once," Samantha complained, but since Steven was kissing the tops of her thighs, her words lacked a certain conviction. "To be fair to Kerry, we should devote an equal amount of time to talking."

"I won't tell her if you won't," Steven murmured as he continued his path of kisses up her body, and by the time he reached her mouth, further discussion was put on hold by mutual consent.

Very late the next morning, Steven stared incredulously over at his wife, whose distractingly lovely and enticingly naked body was propped up next to his on the pillows. "You actually remember something I said to you when you were only ten years old?"

"Word for word," Samantha told him, but after the revelations of last night, the memory of that day no longer had the power to hurt her. "You told the man you were with that my kind of girl was destined to pick up some guy in a bar, marry him and have three kids hanging on her skirts by the time she was twenty. When I lived up to your prediction almost to the letter those words came back to haunt me."

Steven winced as he contemplated his cruel remarks and the effect they'd had on an innocent child. "And that's why you kept putting yourself down around me. You thought I still looked on you that way."

"Yes."

"Please forgive me, Samantha," Steven groaned, overwhelmed by remorse. "I had no idea I'd said anything so hurtful to you. All I remember of that day was that I was fit to be tied. I was so sure that I'd convinced your father to sell, but then he did a complete turnaround on me, and I was forced to go back home with my tail between my legs to report another failure to my dad."

Samantha smiled with compassion. "Caleb just loved to thwart you Armstrongs."

Steven nodded, but his expression was grim. "Yes, he did, but that's no excuse for my taking out my frustrations on you. Now I wish you'd gone and hit me with one of those stones you were always throwing my way."

As she heard the self-reproach in his voice, Samantha felt as if a huge weight had been lifted from her shoulders. Neither one of them could change the past, but it was over, and the future couldn't look any brighter. "I would never have forgiven myself if I'd hit you."

"Why not, I deserved a whole lot worse."

To Steven's astonishment, Samantha leaned over and kissed him full on the mouth. "Once upon a time I would have died before admitting this," she told him, smiling at the befuddled look on his face. "But the only reason I remembered what you'd said to me that day was because I thought you were the most beautiful man I'd ever seen in my life. You rode up to me on that big roan stallion, such a tall, dark and handsome man, and I thought you looked just like Prince Charming."

If anything, her confession made Steven feel even worse. "Well, I did a real fine job of destroying your belief in fairy tales, didn't I?"

Samantha shook her head. "No, Steven. My father and my ex-husband destroyed some of it, but I did the rest myself. Then you came along and kept renewing my faith."

"I did?"

"And not only mine, but my children's as well," Samantha said. "Before you came into our lives, each day seemed like an endless struggle. I was always exhausted and so filled with worry over money that I'd almost forgotten how to laugh. I certainly didn't think I could afford to spend time just having fun. Then you arrived, bringing the kind of fun and laughter my kids were starving for. No wonder they loved you from the first."

"Their mother didn't love me," Steven lamented.

"Their mother was afraid."

"I know," Steven said. "Even when I did my damnedest to reassure you that I wasn't dangerous, you were still scared to death of me."

Samantha laughed at his faulty assumption. "Not of you, but of the feelings you inspired. As soon as I saw you wrapped up in that blanket, I wanted you."

"The hell you say!" Steven exclaimed with a ferocious, disbelieving scowl.

"I did," Samantha insisted. "And then, something even worse happened. I fell in love with you."

"Do you have to make this sound like you contracted the plague?" Steven growled indignantly. "I happen to be both an excellent husband and a terrific lover."

"That was the problem," Samantha informed him. "I thought you were too good to be true. When I found out that you were as wonderful as you acted, I didn't think I deserved you. You gave everything to me, but I had nothing to give back."

"Nothing to give back?" Steven's voice held an angry edge. "All you ever do is give. You're one of the most generous people I've ever met, except when it comes to yourself. I had to fight like hell to get you to take a decent salary when you came to work as my housekeeper!''

"That salary was indecently high, and you know it,'' Samantha declared defensively.

"No, it wasn't, Samantha,'' Steven disagreed. "I paid you the going rate for the job. You just don't have any idea what your skills are worth.''

"Really?'' Samantha scooted up farther on the bed. "You paid your last housekeeper the same thing?''

"Yup,'' Steven said. "And she couldn't even cook.''

"Well, what do you know about that.''

Steven saw the look of amazed delight on her face and shook his head. "I needed you then, Samantha, and I still need you. Your domestic abilities are a plus, but I'd need you even if you didn't know which end of the broom was up. There isn't enough money in the world to pay for what I'm getting in this marriage.''

His vehemence was a balm that removed the last trace of Samantha's fears. "I'm getting a proud, independent, extremely stubborn, loving, beautiful woman to be there when I'm lonely, and love me even when I'm not acting very lovable. I'm getting a woman of integrity and passion whose strengths compensate for my weaknesses, a woman who's proved she isn't afraid to face obstacles and won't quit until she's overcome them. I'm getting more than any man could hope for in his wife.''

"You really believe all that about me, don't you?'' Samantha asked, but her tone made it clear that she didn't need an answer.

Steven pulled her willing body down on top of him. "That and much, much more,'' Steven murmured.

"But there aren't enough words in the English language to describe all I feel."

"Somewhere I heard that if you can't find the right words," Samantha replied thoughtfully, "action works wonders."

"Hmm," Steven murmured as he began a tantalizing trail of kisses down her neck. "Sounds like pretty smart advice to me."

"Me, too," Samantha agreed with a contented sigh. "Me, too."

\*   \*   \*   \*   \*

*Join the enchantment when Robert Armstrong falls under the spell of the lovely Serena Danvers in GYPSY MOON, coming in October from Silhouette Desire.*

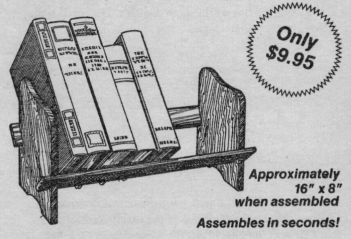

 **Silhouette Desire**

# COMING
# NEXT MONTH

**#445 PASSION'S CHILD—Ann Major**
Book One of the CHILDREN OF DESTINY trilogy!
Amy Holland and Nick Browning's marriage of convenience could
turn to passion—if the secret of their child was not revealed....

**#446 ISLAND HEAT—Suzanne Forster**
When Justin Dunne's search led him to a "haunted castle" and
beautiful Lauren Cambridge, he knew it wasn't the right time to get
involved, unless he could mix business *and* pleasure.

**#447 RAZZMATAZZ—Patricia Burroughs**
Being stranded in the Reno airport left Kennie Sue Ledbetter with
limited options. Alexander Carruthers came to her rescue, and
somehow the next morning she found herself married...to him!

**#448 TRUE COLORS— Mary Blayney**
It would take all of television heartthrob Tom Wineski's considerable
charm to convince small-town single mother Janelle Harper he'd
developed a forever kind of passion.

**#449 A TASTE OF HONEY—Jane Gentry**
Susannah Reid was content with her life...until notorious Jefferson
Cody hit town. He convinced her to start thinking about her own
happiness—not what the neighbors would say.

**#450 ROUGHNECK—Doreen Owens Malek**
Beau Landry was a direct contrast to refined lawyer Morgan Taylor.
Beau had done the wrong thing for the right reason, but when he
proposed, would Morgan approve of his tactics?

# AVAILABLE NOW:

**#439 THE CASTLE KEEP**
Jennifer Greene

**#440 OUT OF THE COLD**
Robin Elliott

**#441 RELUCTANT PARTNERS**
Judith McWilliams

**#442 HEAVEN SENT**
Erica Spindler

**#443 A FRIEND IN NEED**
Cathie Linz

**#444 REACH FOR THE MOON**
Joyce Thies